THE
BURIAL

PANDEM BUCKNER

ISBN: 0692476830
ISBN-13: 978-0692476833 (Twilight Greyce Multimedia)

Also by Pandem Buckner:

Princess Catherine and the Toy Thief (children's book w/Noelle Marie) - the story of Princess Catherine and her friends Seraphee and Puppy, who must rescue their stuffed animal friends from a nefarious toy thief! Armed with nothing but wits and courage, can Princess Catherine save her friends or will they be lost forever?

GIVE: An Anthology of Anatomical Entries (When the Dead Books) – 24 stories of horror, dark humor, and sci-fi, all centered around the theme of organ donation and each written by a different author. Features stories by Christine Morgan, Kerry GS Lipp, Michelle Kilmer, Katie Cord, Pandem Buckner, Jonathan Lambert, and many more.

Lucky's Last Run (coming January 2016 from Evil Girlfriend Media) – sci-fi space opera western told in 80s action-adventure show style. It'll be awesome, just trust me.

Pandem Buckner

CONTENTS

CHAPTER ONE

The call came at 1 PM on Monday, as Luke got ready for work.

Luke Washington shrugged; his white dress shirt felt a little tight across his shoulders. *Might be time for a new one,* he thought as he tucked the shirt into his black slacks, but it was hard to get shirts that fit his shoulders. Next came the cufflinks, a pair of sterling silver racehorses, which Sierra had bought for him after his promotion to assistant manager at the Kentucky Club. As always, he got the first one in just fine, but struggled with the second.

When his cellphone rang, he dropped the cufflink in surprise. He watched as it hit the soft beige carpet and bounced under the dresser, out of easy reach.

"Fuck," he said softly, reaching on top of the dresser for his phone. Plucking it deftly from its place beside his wallet and keys, he checked the screen to see who was calling. The screen read only "Mississippi" and a number that started with 662; he recognized it as his mother's number, calling from her house phone.

"Hello?" He looked under the dresser and found the cufflink, laying just a few inches into the shadows. He also saw one of Sierra's earrings there, one she'd been missing for weeks.

"Hey, Luke," said his mother, Constance, into his ear. Her voice was flat and emotionless, as it always was. "How y'all doin'?"

"Doing okay," Luke replied, stretching his hand out under the dresser as he supported himself on his elbows. "How is everybody there?"

"Well , not too good," Constance said, a hint of some dark emotion – sadness, sorrow, regret; Luke couldn't tell which and was too distracted to try – in her voice. "Got some sad news for you."

Luke's fingers closed, pincer-like, around the cufflink. He dragged it from its hiding place with a satisfied smile. Pressing the phone against his ear with his shoulder, he tried again to put it in place. "What's up?" he asked, knowing that if his mother was calling, someone was either seriously ill or dead.

"Well . . . Billie just called me a little while ago to tell me James passed away today."

"James Jackson?" Luke bent down again to retrieve the earring.

"Yeah - you know he'd been sick with that cancer for a long time." She kept talking, but Luke was no longer paying attention. Reaching for the jewelry box, he'd caught sight of his reflection in the mirror atop the dresser. His smile, his dark eyes, even his slightly pointy ears – all those were traits he'd been told over and over again that he'd gotten from his father.

It didn't seem possible that the source of those traits was dead.

"Luke? Are you there?"

"Yes, Mother, I'm here." Luke dropped the earring into Sierra's jewelry box. The motion felt dreamy to him, unreal; perhaps Constance was mistaken. "What happened to James?"

"Billie said he fell at the house while he was workin' in the yard. One of the neighbors saw him go down and called the ambulance. She was watchin' TV and ain't even know anything was wrong 'til they got there. She said he died on the way to the hospital."

The cufflink finally in place, Luke retrieved his tie from the bed and began tying it – always a half-Windsor knot, like his uncle Werner had taught him – while talking to Constance. The motions felt odd, unreal somehow."Was he cutting the grass? He should have known better than to try anything that strenuous, even in late summer."

"You know how he was, Luke; he thought he could handle everything himself."

"Why didn't Chris do it?"

"Well, you know things wasn't good between them . . ."

3

Things were not better between Luke and James, Luke knew, but at least Christopher had talked to James in the past few years. "Did Billie say when the funeral is going to be?"

"Naw . . . naw, she didn't. I don't know who's gonna be handlin' it all. You know she was about to divorce him."

"I didn't know that," Luke said, pulling the knot tight. The point hung just below his belt, its proper place The routine of dressing felt comforting in this new, James-less reality. Not that James had ever been a large part of Luke's life, but now, even the possibility that he might return was gone.

"Yep, she was - but I'll let her tell you 'bout that, you know I don't like to dabble in other folks' business."

Luke couldn't help smiling at that. While his mother was not as much a matriarch to the family as his grandmother had been, she kept her ears wide open and knew plenty of other folks' business.

"Well," Luke said, reaching for his vest, "I need to get ready for work. I'll give Billie a call tomorrow, find out when the funeral is. Maybe Sierra and I"- Luke smiled a little at the thought of Sierra attending his father's funeral; James would have *loved* that – "will be able to make it down."

"All right, well, tell Sierra I said hi, and let me know what you hear from Billie."

"Okay, Mother, talk to you later."

"Uh-huh. Bye."

4

Luke dropped his phone onto the bed, finished buttoning the vest, and checked himself to make sure everything was in place. He liked wearing white dress shirts; the contrast between them and his mocha-latte skin tones made him look a little bronzed. Formal dress also put some mental distance between himself and Riverton, though he had never admitted that to himself.

James Jackson died today. It still felt unreal.

Luke sat down on the bed, wondering if he'd go to the funeral. He tried not to take much time off, even after becoming the assistant manager, but he knew that Paul, the evening manager, would understand and make sure the hours were covered. Sierra would of course be willing to go. She had tried her best to reach out to his family, with good results – on his mother's side. Luke rarely had anything to do with his father's side of the family, ever since he and James - well. That didn't matter now. There was no point in reliving an argument with a dead man. The Kentucky Club would be fine with him going, Sierra's shop could live without her for a few days, and they could afford the trip, he knew. But was it worth going?

The problem was that he didn't want to go. If he could have asked her, his grandmother would have told him to go. She believed in doing everything that you could for family. While Luke looked up to her greatly, he wondered if she would feel so strongly about James, whom even she didn't like very much. It was something else to think about.

Would Sierra want to go? She'd never met Luke's father, and James had not been a real part of Luke's life in years. He wondered if he should call and tell her, but decided against it. That discussion could wait until after work.

Fatherless. The thought brought back a memory of himself, looking at his birth certificate, several years before; the line where the father's name should have been was blank. That triggered more memories: family barbecues without his father there, Saturday afternoons spent playing outside alone, schools events that his mother attended with no one by her side. *But then again . . . haven't I always been fatherless?*

Luke picked up his shoes from the closet floor, from their usual place, one of three pairs of his shoes next to dozens of Sierra's. They were well-polished and shiny dress shoes, a contrast to James' continually-scuffed sneakers. Luke couldn't help wondering how much of his life was built around not being like his father.

"Fuck," Luke said aloud, then left for work.

****

It was 11:30 when Luke got home again. It had been a slow night at the Kentucky Club, not unusual for a Monday, but even so, there had been the usual little disasters. Royce had badly burned a steak; Emma had accidentally dumped a glass of wine in a patron's lap; Jason had cut his finger on a kitchen knife while he was washing the dishes, and the blood made Rachel shriek. Whatever complaints Luke could make about his job, boredom was not among them.

The TV was off when he stepped into the living room, which struck him as odd: Sierra usually left it on for noise while she went about her evening tasks. Luke wandered around the room, thinking about his father. Where his father had been a messy person, Luke and Sierra's home was neatly organized: the gaming consoles and cable box were all on their own shelves in the entertainment center, various DVDs and Blu-rays alphabetically ordered beneath them. The furniture had been carefully arranged to make the room feel open yet warm, something Luke had never felt that his father was. The only thing out of place in the room was Sierra, who lay stretched out and asleep on the plush sofa.

Luke smiled at seeing her. Her long legs, covered by a blanket, were pointed to the side and slightly bent. Raven curls covered her face, which rested on her arm. Had been she been waiting up for him? He slid off his shoes and crept quietly over to her, moving her hair aside to plant a kiss on her pale cheek.

Her eyes fluttered open at the kiss, revealing green eyes that focused quickly on him. He smiled again, in response to the soft, sleepy smile that graced her well-curved lips. Sierra had a mouth made for smiling; even at rest, the hint of a smile always played about her face.

"Hey baby," she said, her voice heavy with sleep and her deep Southern accent. "How was work?"

"Oh, it was work. Putting out fires as always. How was the shop?" The small used bookstore and café that Sierra ran did more than enough business to sustain itself in a city crowded with both, which was no mean feat.

"It was fine, nothing exciting. Got in some new first editions; I'll look over them tomorrow." Sierra stretched, a motion that never failed to capture Luke's complete attention. He ran his hand along her pajama-covered thigh.

"I'm gonna go take a shower," Luke said, standing up and pulling off his tie. "You coming up to bed?"

"Yeah, just let me straighten the kitchen up. I'll be there by the time you get out of the shower." Sierra stood with him, kissed him softly on the lips, and walked off to the kitchen. Luke watched her walk away, then went upstairs for his shower.

When he got out of the shower, Sierra was already in bed, snuggled beneath the sheets. Luke, clad only in a t-shirt and silk boxers, pulled back the blankets and climbed into both the bed and her waiting arms.

"I missed you today," she said, kissing his cheek.

"I missed you too," Luke replied, kissing her cheek in return and snuggling close against her throat. He wondered how to break the news to her. She'd care, of course, but given what happened with her father, would she understand? He regretted not having told her much about James.

"What's on your mind?" Sierra asked, her fingers running over his close-cropped curly hair.

"What makes you think something's on my mind?"

Sierra chuckled in response. "Please. I know without looking you've got that dark look again. What's wrong?"

Luke sighed. "My mother called today."

Sierra turned around, squeezed him tight to her bosom, and resumed stroking his hair. "What's wrong?"

"My . . . father died." Luke barely managed to choke out the words.

"Oh! Oh, Luke, I'm so sorry," Sierra said, squeezing him close again then moving back to look into his eyes. "I know you two weren't close, but still. When is the funeral?"

"I don't know. It doesn't matter, anyway. I'm not going," he said quietly.

"Why not?" Sierra let him go and sat up on her elbows, looking down into his face. "Funerals are really for the living, you know; they're all about closure and goodbyes. No matter what happened, he was still your father."

"As far as that goes, yeah, but it's not like he was ever really there for me. He bought my first car, but never came to any of my awards ceremonies or plays. He sent me money when he was out of town, but never taught me how to shave or played catch with me or taught me how to talk to women. He came to my high school graduation, the only one he came to for any of his children, and I hated that he did that." The argument felt like a weak excuse to Luke, a thin cover for his just simply not wanting to go. "I don't owe him anything. None of us do."

"No, I know, you don't." Sometimes I wonder if his negligence was worse than *my* father's attention." Sierra's eyes grew dark.

"Not being abusive doesn't really make up for not being there at all."

"So be a better man than him and be there for him, even though he wasn't for you?" She had a point, he had to admit.

"I guess that's one way to look at it." Luke put his arms around Sierra and pulled her head down to his chest. He hadn't meant to bring up painful memories of her abusive father. Fathers were rarely discussed in their house, since neither of them had anything resembling positive paternal relationships. As she maintained her silence on hers, he had likewise kept quiet about his.

"What happened? What kept you two from being close?"

"When I was little, it was probably his other kids. Oh, and his wife. Then he ran into . . . some trouble and had to leave town for a few years. When he came back, I was 18 and about to leave for college."

"But you two got along better when you were in college, you said. He sent you money, helped you get a place when you dropped out - what happened after that? You never would tell me."

"We had an argument." Luke paused, unsure of how to phrase what happened. In the impatient silence, he decided it best to just blurt it out, no sugarcoating. "He didn't think it was 'safe,' his word, for me to have so many white friends."

Sierra arched an eyebrow at Luke. "Really?" Luke nodded. "Wow. But that was what, nine years ago? That's a long time for neither of you to not even try to-"

"There was something else." Luke sighed. He should have told her sooner about this, always meant to, but somehow just never got around to it. If he was honest with himself, not telling her before had more to do with being ashamed of James than any lapse of memory. "Remember when we told my mother we were engaged?"

"Of course I do," Sierra replied with a smile. "She cooked a fantastic dinner!"

"I saw him then, when I went out for groceries." Luke remembered that meeting, the last time they'd ever spoken. Of course, he hadn't know that it would be the last time; he couldn't help wondering how it would have gone if he'd known. "I went to Billie's house – he had married her by then – to tell him the good news."

Sierra's smile disappeared. "And? Why didn't you tell me about it?"

"Because of what he said. I didn't want you to be hurt by it."

"What did he say?" No smile on her face now, just firm-set lips expecting something unpleasant.

"He said he'd be damned if his son married a white woman."

Sierra didn't reply. There was nothing to say to that, and both of them knew it. Eventually, they slept, but Luke was unsure who fell asleep first.

****

With his bald head, muscular frame, and well-groomed moustache, Paul Cussler sometimes seemed to Luke more like a biker than a restaurant manager, but Luke had to admit he was great at being a manager, and generally a good friend. Plus, he looked completely natural in his black work suit.

Around them, the Kentucky Club was largely empty. The huge back bar ran nearly the length of the narrow bottom floor, carved in a horse-racing motif with horses' heads at the ends that looked almost like gargoyles. Between the heads, a horse race was carved into the top. The back bar was solid mahogany and very old; it had been carved in the early 1900s and would, Luke thought, probably outlast the restaurant. Ornate oak stools continued the motif, with their backs carved to look like racing flags. On the wall opposite the bar hung framed pictures of the Club's most famous and infamous patrons, most of them signed. Bill Clinton, Barack Obama, Kevin Costner, Bill Gates, Jeff Bezos, and others watched as Paul and Luke prepped the bar for the evening's trade.

"So you're really not gonna go?" Paul asked, checking the liquid level in the bottles.

"Nope," Luke said as he checked the beer taps. "No real point in it, is there? It's not like we were close at all."

"Yeah, but . . . he was your *dad*, you know? That's gotta hurt, even if you weren't close. Besides, funerals give closure, right? Go get some closure, put him behind you, and move on."

"Sierra said the same thing," Luke chuckled – and the sound reminded him again of James Jackson. "It's not just that we weren't close, not really. It's just, well, he was kind of a shitheel, too."

"How so?" Paul ducked into the liquor closet beside the stairs. Luke raised his voice to be heard over the clinking of bottles.

"He had eight kids by three different women, only one of whom was his wife, and didn't do shit for any of them."

"Didn't you say-"A bottle of vodka toppled out of Paul's arms; Luke caught it and put it behind the bar. "Thanks. Didn't you say he bought your first car? That doesn't sound too bad to me."

"Yeah, he did, and that little bit is more than he ever gave any of his other children. It kinda caused problems between them and me – and between him and me, once I grew up and realized how unfair it was to his other kids."

"Ohhhhhhhh." The word was a drawn-out exhale. "Yeah, I can see how that might make things a little unpleasant. But you should still go, Luke. You *need* to go. Trust me." Paul put a hand on Luke's shoulder. His eyes were more intense than Luke could remember them ever being before. "It's important to get that closure. You might regret it if you go, but if you *don't* go, I promise you'll regret it later. Speaking from experience here: grief takes a toll, even if you don't think it will."

"Sierra said pretty much the same, but-" Luke's phone rang. Automatically, he reached into his vest pocket and pulled it out; the number started with 662, his mother's area code in Mississippi, but was otherwise unfamiliar to him. "Hmm. I should probably take this."

"All right, I'll get the tills set up, then we'll be ready for another fun Tuesday. You need to go to that funeral, Luke. I'm serious."

"I'll think about it," Luke replied, mostly to appease Paul, as he headed into the liquor closet. The dimly-lit, cramped, dusty closet barely had enough room for him to stand upright between the racks of bottles, but it was private. "Hello?"

"Yes, is this Luke Washington?"

"Yes it is, who is this?"

A smooth voice, polite but not very warm, replied. "Mr. Washington. My name is Doctor Torres; I'm with Queen's Sons Hospital, in Riverton, Mississippi."

"Ummm . . . hello, Dr. Torres. What's up?" Luke's heartbeat sped up; had something happened to Constance? Or Rebekah? Why hadn't Werner or anyone else called him first? It couldn't be about James; surely somebody else was handling all that.

"Well, I'm calling about your father, James Jackson."

"What about him? I heard he died yesterday; did he get back up and grope a nurse?"

Dr. Torres laughed, then stifled it. "No, nothing like that. He's still quite dead. No, this is a different problem."

"Okay," Luke said, puzzled. "What is it?"

Luke could hear Dr. Torres sigh deeply on the other end of the line. "Mr. Washington, someone needs to take responsibility for the body. I need to know what funeral home to release him to, someone needs to come pick up his personal effects. I was told you might be willing to do that."

"By who? Dr. Torres, you might not be aware of this, but I'm in Seattle. I'm kind of far away to handle paperwork. Maybe you could find someone closer?"

Dr. Torres sighed again; Luke read it as the sigh of someone who's had to do this sort of thing before and hated it every time. "Mr. Washington, you are the ninth person I've called, *including* his widow. I've been through this before, and I know what'll happen. If you turn me down, I'm going to have to give Mr. Jackson's body over to the county as a transient. They'll just cremate him on the cheap and his ashes will sit in a plastic box on a shelf in a funeral home until someone claims him or they figure out a legal way to dispose of them."

Luke visualized what Dr. Torres had described. It seemed far more terrible than death to be left on a shelf somewhere, forgotten, unwanted, unloved. "Nobody else was willing to take responsibility?"

"Nobody, Mr. Washington, nobody at all. I've been here for twenty years and never seen a person with so many family and friends that nobody wanted to deal with." Dr. Torres took a deep breath, then resumed his formal tone. "This is my last call, Mr. Washington; my next call is to the county. Will you do this, or not?"

Luke was silent. He didn't *want* to do this. What had his father, who figured in his life as little more than his mother's chosen sperm donor, done to earn Luke's efforts in this? He had never attended a school play, never beamed over a report card, never even played catch with Luke. Paul had just said Luke needed to go, that he would regret if it he didn't go, but what was one more regret?

Slowly, the silence filled with words, spoken in a familiar female voice, rich in passion. "We do for family." Luke's grandmother's motto. She'd said it like it was written in stone and brought down the mountain by Moses himself. Luke didn't want to go to the funeral, didn't want to go back to Riverton – but what would his grandmother have thought? What would she have done?

All the reasons he had given Paul, all the reasons he'd given to Sierra, all of the ones he'd held close to his chest: those reasons were still in force. Whatever his reasons, he really didn't want to go. He didn't want to go back to Riverton, he really didn't want to deal with his family, he didn't want to leave *his* life to deal with James' death.

But he remembered his grandmother's voice, saying, "We do for family." The way she'd done for him, for the family she'd brought together, the people whose lives she'd touched whether they were blood family or friends. He remembered her words as clearly as if she was saying them now. Whatever else James had been, he'd been family – and nobody else was doing anything.

"We do for family."

"Mr. Washington, I need an answer now. Will you do it?"

Luke sighed. "Get a pen and paper, Dr. Torres. I'll tell you where to fax the paperwork."

CHAPTER TWO

"Everything's good so far. I'm in the car now – it's a nice one, a Nissan something-or-other, sedan, very comfy." Luke adjusted the air conditioner to a higher setting. Seattle had been cool, but the afternoon heat of early fall Arkansas, though familiar, required a little mechanical adjustment.

"Are you sure about doing this alone? Dawn can handle the shop without me for a few days. " There was no reason to subject Sierra to all the bullshit he would have to deal with in Riverton. Besides, she needed to stay behind for her shop - and, of course, her houseplants.

"No, I can do this," Luke replied. He didn't want Riverton tainting Sierra, dragging her into its miasma of sadness. "I think it's better I do this alone." Luke navigated the car swiftly out of the airport lot, following the signs for Highway 65 South, which he knew from memory would take him to Lake Village. There he would connect with Highway 82, which would take him east, into Greenville, Mississippi. From there, he'd take Highway 1 south to Riverton.

"If you're sure."

"I am. I'd better hang up and drive, dear, I'm getting on Highway 65."

"Okay. Drive safely, baby. Love you."

"Love you too. I'll call you later." Luke hung up and removed his earpiece. He'd called Constance from the Little Rock Airport to let her know he'd landed, so she knew he'd be there in about four hours. Having called Sierra as well, all his communication was done. The next few hours belonged to him and the open road.

Luke loved to travel, but rarely had the opportunity to do so. He remembered his first airplane ride, to Washington, DC; he had laughed in joy and excitement as the plane taxied down the runway. Driving had a pleasure of its own as well. The solitude and freedom to think, the steel ballet of cars on the highway, even stopping at convenience stores for bad food: he loved every part of traveling. That came from James, Constance had told Luke. While Luke loved travel, he could not remember the last time Constance had left Riverton without a funeral or a doctor's visit to go to.

Luke didn't want to think about James or Constance right now. He'd be dealing with plenty of their shit soon.

Instead, he looked in the rearview and saw the semi-skyscrapers of Little Rock fading in the distance. He remembered thinking of Little Rock as "the big city" when he was young, and chuckled. The sound reminded him again that he had inherited his father's laugh. There was just no getting away from James.

To distract himself from that memory, Luke consciously thought about all the trips he'd taken along this highway, some of them fond memories, some not so fond, until a particular crossroads caught his eye. Luke smiled as he passed the turnoff that led to Arkadelphia, where he'd gone to college. He'd never brought Sierra back to see his old collegiate haunts; he would one day. Arkadelphia was one of his favorite places in the world; maybe she would like it as well.

Pine Bluff was the largest city on the route until he hit Greenville; everything between would be one- and two-stoplight towns, usually about 15 minutes apart. It was so unlike the Seattle area, where one found solid city from Olympia to Marysville. And you'd never see a tractor on the main highways there, he reflected as he passed a farmer driving a John Deere on the shoulder. Luke waved, and the farmer, to Luke's surprise, waved back. *I'd forgotten how much friendlier the people are here.*

As Luke drove, the small towns got fewer and further between. The emptiness freed his mind to wander and remember old times. He entered Star City, where he and a friend crashed a house party in high school and nearly got beaten up. McGehee came and went; Constance had brought him there once to meet James while he was still a truck driver. He passed the turn off of the main highway to Montrose, where a girl had broken his high school heart.

Luke pulled up to the one red light in Lake Village, where Highway 82 joined Highway 65 for a few miles before veering off towards Eudora, leaving 82 to journey alone across the river and into Mississippi. There was the same gas station on the corner, the same package store on another corner – he remembered being told in school that one could see seven liquor stores from that intersection, but had never tested the information – a tractor dealership on another corner, and on the last, another gas station. They hadn't changed at all since Luke was 10. In Seattle, there was always construction: new buildings going up, old ones being torn down. His adopted city was constantly in flux, but his home stomping grounds seemed to be in stasis.

"I wonder, which way is really better?" Luke said aloud.

The car, and the road, did not answer.

****

Riverton.

An old city, it had been there since before the Revolutionary War, and of no strategic importance to either side. In the 1830s, it had been flooded with new Italian immigrants, who ran there to flee the oppression and discrimination they'd faced on the East Coast. Those families bought up most of the farmland, aided by an 1836 earthquake that scared away many of the previous settlers and changed the course of the Mississippi River. The descendants of those brave Italians still held most of the land, having rarely sold even a small parcel of land to developers or people seeking their own homes. As a result of all the land being in the hands of a few families, the area was desperately poverty-stricken, with not many economic opportunities available. Most of the people in Riverton that had jobs either worked for the government or commuted to Jackson, Greenville, or even Hattiesburg for work. The rest did seasonal work on the farms, or drank and smoked their sorrows away and subsisted on the kindness of taxpayers and family members.

Riverton was not a hopeful place.

Coming into the small city, Luke was not at all surprised to see that what little traffic there was consisted of people going in the opposite direction, out of town. They were, he surmised, most likely heading to Greenville to work at the factories there or to play at the casinos, or towards Jackson for third shift at the Nissan plant, or to Tunica, for the bigger casinos there.

It's my hometown, Luke thought. *So why has it never felt like home?* He couldn't answer that question. He'd just never felt like he fit in, not even with his own family; that was probably the answer, but it never felt like a *complete* answer.

Luke passed through the city, passed by the sparse homes and buildings scattered across the farmland, until they began to cluster tighter together and finally formed Riverton proper. Highway 1 was the main road through town, and, after the first red light, only businesses fronted the four-lane highway. Luke knew them all pretty well: the grocery stores, the department stores, the liquor stores, tamale stands, fast-food restaurants – all of them had been his world once.

At the south end of town, on Luke's right, stood the Riverton Mall, a one-story collection of 15 or 16 stores. The parking lot that surrounded the building was half-full; Luke wondered if today had been payday or check day. It had changed a little since his last visit: the family-owned restaurant that stood at the east entrance had been replaced by an Applebee's. Some people called that progress; Luke would not have counted himself among them.

After the mall, the buildings petered out again. A few miles on, he found the turnoff to Luze Road, which was unlit and straddled by acres of farmland. He drove slowly over the potholed road, knowing it could be death on cars driven by the unwary, but it seemed that not even the potholes had changed much since his last visit. Two miles down that road, then the right turn to Framer's Point, and three more miles . . . there, in the middle of nowhere, the farm.

Luke pulled over to the gravel-and-grass shoulder of Framer's Point Road at the top of an incline and got out, walking quickly to his right. Ten yards in front of him stood one pecan tree, separated from the dozen or so in the pecan orchard across the road behind him. It maintained a lonely vigil over a two-acre patch of grass dotted with headstones. He stopped before one, knelt, and placed flowers he'd picked up at a convenience store on the grave.

"Hello, Grandma," he said. "I know, it's been a while. I'm sorry."

No answer came except a slight breeze whispering between the headstones.

"I'm doing okay. I'm an assistant manager at the Kentucky Club now. It definitely pays a lot better but it's a lot more stress. Sierra's bookshop is doing pretty good. She says it's a headache to run, but she always smiles when she says it. You liked her smile; I remember you said so, the first time you met her. She's not with me today. I came back alone."

Luke sighed.

"No, no kids yet. Sierra can't have children. We gave up trying after the second miscarriage, it's just not going to happen. I think we'll probably adopt in a couple of years, once the bookshop is more stable and I've gotten a raise or two. That way we'll have a more comfortable financial situation. I don't want to be like - well, to have to struggle and worry."

A faint sound, wood scraping against wood, caught Luke's attention. He glanced around, but couldn't find its source. He shrugged and continued.

"You're right, I'm avoiding the real topic. You probably already know this, but . . . James died Monday. I don't know if you two ended up in the same place – actually, I kinda doubt it. Anyway, he's dead, and I wasn't going to come back for the funeral, but.... Nobody wanted to take care of him. The doctor told me I was the ninth person he'd called, and if I didn't take care of it, he was going to call the county and have him cremated. They'd cremate him and put him on a shelf somewhere ... until somebody picked him up, or ... or until they could ... legally throw him away."

A hitching in Luke's chest interrupted him. He paused to let it subside, before it turned into tears, then went on.

"I just couldn't let them do that. That's got to be the saddest thing in the world, right? Sitting on a shelf, forgotten and unwanted, even though you're just a pile of bone char and ashes and don't eat and don't do anything but just sit there in a plastic box. That just - it makes me so sad. I wouldn't want to end up like that. James wasn't Father of the Year, any year; really, not even in the running. To be honest, he was closer to the other end of the list - but nobody deserves *that*. Nobody deserves to be forgotten. So I came back to take care of him, because like you always said: we do for family. And nobody else was doing anything."

Another faint sound, this time like pieces of wood slamming together, came to Luke's ears. He looked south, across a field of greens and down the incline, between pine and magnolia trees, to his grandmother's house about forty yards away. This time, he saw, albeit just barely, the curtains behind the window in Constance's room draw shut.

"I guess Mother knows I'm here," Luke said, standing up. "I'd better get down there. You know how she gets." Luke kissed the tips of his fingers, then touched them to the rose-marble headstone. "Goodbye, Grandma. I love you."

Luke touched his face as he turned away from the headstone, only slightly surprised to find tears there, and wiped them away.

Looking to the northeast, he could see Gethsemane Baptist Church a half mile away. It had been founded over a hundred years before by his great-grandfather, owned and operated by the family ever since. The church was usually unoccupied until Sunday, so Luke was surprised to see a pickup truck parked in front. In the evening light, he couldn't make out whose it was, but figured Constance would know.

"Okay," he said. "I gotta go."

A breeze blew through the cemetery as Luke walked back to his car, stirring the few fallen leaves, and rustling those still attached to the lonely pecan tree.

****

Just past the huge white mailbox, Luke turned off of Framer's Point Road onto the gravel driveway. He turned right at the fork in the driveway; the left path led into the fields. The same tractors he'd grown up with were parked in the fields, waiting to be driven out to harvest and plow when needed. He parked behind his mother's car, an old Chevy Malibu. Next to it sat a relatively new Nissan Altima, only four or five years old, but already heavily dinged and, as he could smell when he got out of his car, leaking oil to boot. Rebekah had never been easy on cars; that too had not changed. Even the garage doors were still rusted open.

The dog that barked at him as he walked into the garage *was* new, however. White with a large brown spot covering its back, a smaller one on its snout and partially covering one eye, and black feet, it barked as though it was far bigger than the maybe-twelve-inches it stood at the shoulder. Luke paused, considering what to do about it. As he pondered, the door opened and Constance filled the doorway.

"BINGO! Hush, Bingo, it's just Luke," she said, pointing at the dog. Bingo laid his ears flat against his head and laid down beside the single step up to the door, a chastised look on his face as he resumed gnawing a bone. "That's Bingo, Luke. He's a pretty good guard dog." Constance stepped back as Luke stepped over the dog and into the kitchen.

"Where did Bingo come from?" Luke asked, though he figured he already knew the answer. The kitchen was the same as he remembered it - a counter running parallel with the unpredictable-at-best stove for about half the length of the room, until it stopped at the washing machine and dryer. Next to the dryer sat a junk-filled corner; the junk looked to be exactly the same junk it had been on his last visit, if a bit dustier. Down the wall from the stove sat an antique Singer sewing machine table, looking somehow majestic and historic even under all the dirt, and with the sewing machine folded inside. An old, worn-looking microwave oven sat on top of the Singer. Luke remembered the day they got that microwave; he had been excited about having microwave popcorn for the first time. Either the microwave was now 20 years old, or Constance had replaced the old one with another just like it. If it was the same microwave, Luke reckoned it was probably still the youngest appliance in the kitchen.

"Oh, you know, he just showed up one day. I needed a dog, so I kep' him." Luke did indeed know. Nearly all of his childhood pets had been obtained in a similar fashion: someone had a pet they didn't want, so they dropped it off in the country and probably told their kids it was living on a farm somewhere. Some of them made their way to the Washington farm, and lived there for the rest of their days – until they died of wolves, coyotes, hunters, or just sickness. Constance refused to ever take an animal to see a vet. "Was the drive all right?"

"Yeah, it was fine," Luke said, following his mother to his right, into the dining room. A solid oak eight-person table dominated the room, with another sewing machine table and a china hutch at the opposite end. An antique chandelier hung above the table. Luke could count the number of times the whole family had actually eaten together at that table on one hand, but it looked nice nonetheless.

"So how come Sierra didn't come with you?" Constance asked, passing through the dining room and into the living room. His grandmother's chair, which he could not yet think of as Constance's, as only death had removed his grandmother from that chair, was to his left as he entered the living room. A table and couch filled most of one wall; an old window-unit air conditioner and a fireplace dominated the other, with a picture window running from the fireplace to the hallway. A third antique Singer table sat before the window, covered with potted houseplants: aloe vera, African violets, some others he couldn't identify. If they weren't the same plants his grandmother cared for, they were certainly descendants of those plants, living in the same pots like children who had never left home.

"Oh, she was busy with the bookstore. It's doing pretty good. She's been doing well with rare books, and they bring in a lot of money." Luke looked around at the cobwebs in the corners, wondering if the spiders too had been there since his childhood.

Constance dropped down into the recliner. Her black hair, a genetic holdover from their Native ancestors, was streaked with grey and cut short, framing her circular brown face. That had been Rebekah's idea, Luke figured. Left to her own devices, his mother would have worn her hair in a ponytail every single day of her life. Even with the weight she had gained over the years rounding out her short frame, she still looked younger than her sixty years. The slump of her shoulders, however, was new to Luke, as was the increased thickness of her large, round-framed glasses. "Oh well. Maybe she'll come down next time."

"Maybe," Luke replied, taking a seat on the closest end of the couch. *All right, out with it, let's get it over with, Mother.*

"I saw you stopped over at the cemetery," Constance said, lifting a cup from the table to her lips. "You coulda come here first. The dead ain't goin' nowhere."

Around here, the living don't seem to be going anywhere either. He barely stopped himself from speaking the words.

This conversation might turn into a fight, but Luke wasn't going to be the one that started it. "Well, you know, it's just kinda like ritual now: stop in, see Grandma, then come up to her house." He winced as soon as the words were out of his mouth, but it was too late to take them back.

Constance sighed as she set her cup back onto the table. "I guess so. Just make some time for the livin', all right?"

"I always do," Luke said. "How's retirement?"

"Oh, it's fine, it's just fine. Nothing much to do all day 'cept watch TV. At least with that satellite, I get enough channels to keep it interestin'." They didn't have cable or satellite TV when Luke was growing up; just an antenna that got four channels – five, if weather permitted. "Luke, where's your suitcase?"

"At the hotel." His suitcase was outside in the car, but having an argument about staying at the house was greatly preferable to actually staying at the house.

"Oh, Luke, you didn't have to spend no money on a hotel. You coulda stayed here."

"With you, Rebekah, and Matthew here, where would I sleep? I didn't know if Rebekah's kids were going to be here or not, and they sleep in the spare room."

"You coulda slept on my bed, I woulda slept on the couch."

Luke just barely managed not to roll his eyes. "It's okay, Mother. The hotel has internet access, and that's kinda spotty out here."

"Internet access is worth that much?"

"Yeah, to me. I'm still writing, and I keep in touch with a lot of people by email, so it's kind of important." Luke hated to lie, but it was easier than an argument. The spare room was filled to the brim with Rebekah's crap. The hotel would be much quieter, and neater, with fewer poisonous snakes around and internet access that was wi-fi rather than dial-up. Explaining his aesthetic reasons to Constance, however, would only have given her something to argue against.

"All right then," Constance said, settling back into the chair with a long-suffering sigh. "So when's the funeral? Billie never did call me back about it."

"I don't know yet, probably Saturday. I'm meeting with Tim Marston tomorrow at Kirkman."

"*You* are?" Constance raised her eyebrow at him. "Why are *you* meeting with him?"

Luke sighed deeply, tired of having to explain why. He hated few things so much as repeating himself, and he didn't think Constance would listen as much as Sierra and Paul had. "Because nobody else would handle it. A doctor called me from the hospital and told me that if I didn't take care of James, he was gonna give him to the county. He faxed me the paperwork, had me sign it and send it back, and he released the body to Kirkman's. Tim took the call."

"How is ol' Tim? I ain't seen him in a long time."

"He sounded all right." Luke looked up at the corners of the room. The cobwebs were still there, seemingly abandoned by long-dead arachnids.

"So why you, Luke?"

The upright piano in the corner was missing a key. He'd fallen and knocked it out at least two decades ago. The key was still sitting on top of the piano, waiting for someone to try to fix it. "Because my name was last in the phone book?"

"If Billie wasn't willin' to handle it, and his family wasn't, you should have left that alone." The words came out of Constance with a righteous finality, as if differing opinions were completely irrelevant.

Luke sighed again "Somebody had to, Mother. I was the last person he could call."

For a second, Luke thought he saw irritation on his mother's face. "Well . . . I don't know, I just don't think you shoulda gotten involved."

"Well, you're welcome to go to the arrangements tomorrow with me. Tim told me to bring anybody that might want to help me plan things out."

"Oh, Luke, I don't think so. You know him and me wasn't close."

Not with the lights on, anyway. Though he didn't say the words aloud, the bitter sarcasm in his head rankled him. Did he really expect to be attacked so badly that he was already mentally sniping at others? "I don't want to have to do it all myself. I've never arranged anybody's funeral before."

"I don't think so, Luke—" Outside, a car door slammed. "Huh, Werner must be done at the church."

Proving her words, Werner strode into the living room moments later, with his customary statement of presence. "Hey there," he said, then saw Luke. "Luke! How you doin', boy?" His long legs covered the walk to the couch in two steps, barely enough time for Luke to stand up and nearly get crushed in a tight hug.

"Uhhhhhh," Luke said, trying to regain his breath. His uncle might have been in his late 60s, but he was apparently still strong as hell. Luke stood back and looked at Werner. Tall, but still solid, Werner looked completely natural in worn jeans and a faded plaid button-up shirt. His darkened skin told the tale of his work outdoors as a handyman and carpenter, while the muscles beneath spoke of his indoor job as a steelworker. His mustache, which framed his wide white smile and continued down to his chin, was immaculately groomed, as was his hair, though a lot had been lost to baldness. "I'm doing good, Uncle Werner, or at least I was when I still had unbroken ribs."

"Ha!" Werner said, and gripped Luke's shoulder. "Don't let that city make you soft, boy! Hey, where's your wife?"

"She couldn't make it this trip - this was kind of unexpected."

"He's here to make arrangements for James' funeral," Constance cut in.

"Aw, yeah. I was sorry to hear 'bout that." Werner stepped back and let Luke sit down.

"Thanks," Luke replied, feeling a bit steadier.

Werner turned to Constance. "The grass at the church is cut; I'm headin' on back into town. Ya'll need anything?"

"Naw, we're good, thanks. Tell Della I said hi."

"Okay. Luke, good to see you, I'll see you again before you go, right?"

"Yeah, you will. I'll try to get by and see you and Della before I go." Della was Werner's wife, a perfect Southern hostess who always made Luke feel welcome in her home.

"All right. See ya'll later," Werner said, and left.

Constance and Luke sat in silence for a moment, until a "hey" from the hallway punctured the distance between them. Luke turned to see his brother Matthew standing in the hallway.

"Hey, Matthew."

"Hey. Who was here? I thought I heard a voice." Matthew was built like Luke, with the same mocha skin, the same freckles, hair, and eyes – or perhaps it was more accurate that Luke was built like Matthew, since Matthew was the older of the two by five years. Matthew was also taller and skinnier, due more to being diabetic than any deliberate attempt at weight maintenance.

"Werner was here but he left," Constance said. His curiosity satisfied, Matthew turned to go back to his room.

"Hey wait," Luke said. "I don't suppose you'd like to help me arrange a funeral for James tomorrow, would you Matthew had tried to cause this funeral ten years ago, but Luke saw no point in bringing that up now.

Matthew glared at Luke, then turned back to the hallway and disappeared around the corner.

"I guess not," Luke said, settling back into the couch.

"Don't mess with your brother like that. You know he didn't like James."

"I know. I was there when he proved it, remember?" Luke instantly regretted the sharp tone of his words, and tried to make his next ones more conciliatory. "I guess I was hoping he might have forgiven James already, but maybe I was wrong."

"You were," Constance said.

"Where's Rebekah?"

"In her bedroom taking a nap. I think she's going out later tonight." Constance looked up at the ceiling as she spoke, as if a prayer was hidden in the words.

"On a weeknight? Doesn't she have work tomorrow?"

"Yeah, she does, but she'll still be going out after she borrows some money from me. I just finished paying her car note too." From her expression, Luke didn't think an outside observer could have been blamed for thinking that payment required donating an organ.

"I don't understand how she's had the same job for 15 years-"

"Don't start, Luke. Just leave it alone." She made a dismissive gesture with one hand, shooing his words away.

"Right," Luke said, standing up. "I should get back to the hotel. It's been a long day, with the flight and the drive and all."

"Okay," Constance said, getting up to walk him to the door. "You comin' out tomorrow?"

"Yeah," Luke replied as they walked. "I'm gonna try to get hold of Billie and Chris first, though, see if I can talk them into helping."

"Well, good luck. Billie was about to divorce James, you know, and Chris wasn't too happy with him either."

They reached the back door, the same door Luke had entered through. "Why was she about to kick him out, anyway?"

"She said he cheated on her," Constance said, a sadness in her eyes that Luke couldn't place.

Luke reached for the misshapen doorknob. "Given that he cheated on his first wife with her," - *and you*, he omitted - "she really should have seen that coming."

"They say a leopard never changes his spots, but that don't stop people from hopin' they will. See you tomorrow, Luke."

Pandem Buckner

CHAPTER THREE

"So just the basics?"

"Yeah, Tim, please." Luke braced himself for the sticker shock.

"Obituary, wake, funeral, burial plot, body care – that's what we call embalmin' and pickin' 'em up and shit – then the pastor's fee, hearse, grave liner, family limo, all that ol' shit . . . come out to – hang on, let me check – come out to $7,915.39."

"What the *fuck*?" Shocked that "the basics" cost so much, Luke rocked back in his chair, slapping his palms on the oval table.

"*Shhhhhhh*, nigga, I told you, I got a headache," Tim Marston replied, his eyes narrowing to slits. He took a sip from his coffee thermos; Luke thought he could smell something alcoholic mixed in with the coffee. Try as he might, though, he couldn't be sure that the scent of booze wasn't actually coming out of Tim's pores. Tim did seem a little unhealthy, a thin sheen of sweat covering his dark chocolate skin and thin mustache, but Luke had always known Tim to be a heavy drinker. It stood to reason that the headache was more hangover than illness.

"Right, right, sorry," Luke said, lowering his voice, "but *eight thousand dollars*? You know I ain't buryin' the mayor , right?"

"Those are family prices too, nigga. Dyin' is fuckin' *expensive*, lemme tell you." Tim took another sip. "It wasn't James that died, we'd be talkin' twelve, thirteen thousand, easy. But he was my cousin, ya heard? We was *family*, even if we wasn't close family. I remember he took me to a party one night when I was 15 - James got me my first piece a'pussy *and* my first drink at that party. I owed that nigga a lot, ya know? So I'm doin' what I can for him, 'cause I loved him, and what I can for you, 'cause I love *you* too, even though you can't ever call your cousin and say hi like a *normal* motherfucka."

"Is this how you talk in every arrangement?"

"Hell no! I ain't that stupid." Tim shuffled some papers in front of him, placed them back onto the table, and seemed to regain some of his composure. "But this is what I can do for you. I can't do no better, Luke."

Luke looked around. The table could seat six people easily, but he and Tim were the only ones there. No one else sat at the table, no one wandered the back of the room, looking at the mounted casket models. Just himself, and Tim, seated at the table at the head of the room, the double doors behind him, Tim across from him. Though Luke had tried, he couldn't get anyone else to come to the arrangement. After Constance and Billie had both said no,

Billie's refusal over the phone after he got to the hotel, Luke gave up and came alone.

No one wanted to help make funeral plans for his father.

And he severely doubted that anyone would want to help pay for it.

Luke stared down at the plush beige carpet. It looked new.

"Well?"

"Tim, I don't *have* eight thousand dollars sitting around."

In response, Tim scratched his chin. "Well.... Did James have insurance? We take payments from insurance plans."

"He didn't have a job, and if he had any insurance, I'm pretty sure the cancer took care of it."

"What about Billie?" Tim slurped down the last of his coffee as Luke shrugged noncommittally. "Constance? Yo' brothers and sisters?"

"Good fucking luck to me on getting them to give anything."

"You better fuckin' try," Tim replied, slurping down the last of whatever had been in his Thermos. "This shit gotta be paid."

"I figured that." Luke stood up. "I'll see what I can do."

"Yeah, man, you do that," Tim said, wobbling to his feet. "Just get back to me by 6. I gotta get the obituary in to the paper tonight if they're gonna run it tomorrow."

"Shit," Luke said, smacking his forehead as he and Tim walked out of the arrangement room. "I forgot to get some obit info from Billie."

"Oh, yeah, yeah, I need that too. Hey, I got some stuff you need to take to her, by the way."

Luke raised his eyebrow and stopped in the portrait-lined hallway. "Stuff like what?"

"What?" Tim looked at him and laughed. "Naw, not stuff like *that*. I mean personal effects and shit. James's wallet, the clothes he had on, shit like that."

"Oh, okay," Luke said, and kept walking.

Tim tapped Luke's shoulder. "Hey, see if she got a suit of his to put him in. If she ain't got one, you might have to buy one."

"All right," Luke said. They stopped at the door to the office. Tim stepped inside, then shuffled back out with a plastic bag. Luke saw folded clothes and a pair of grass-dotted tennis shoes inside the bag.

"Here you go," Tim said, handing the bag to Luke. "Take that to Billie when you go see her, and get back to me when you want, as long as it's before 6."

"Will do, Luke said, looking at the bag. He didn't *want* to go to Billie's house. He didn't *want* to be here, handling arrangements for his dead father alone. For the hundredth time, he reminded himself that he had chosen to be here.

The glass doors of Kirkman Memorial Services closed softly behind him.

****

"Well, hey, Luke! Gimme a hug, boy!"

Billie's slender arms reached out beyond her doorframe and wrapped around Luke. He embraced her gently in return, her salt-and-pepper hair tickling his nose as they hugged. She felt less substantial than she had the last time they'd hugged, years before; he chalked it up to age stealing some of her vibrancy. "Hey, Billie."

"Let me get a look at you," she said, standing back, her hands on his shoulders. As she took him in, Luke did the same with her. She was as slender as she had always been, though the paunch around her middle was new. Her hair also seemed wispier and thinner than it had before, and her skin, always the color of a chocolate bar, seemed to hang sallow in places. Her teeth, yellowed from years of smoking, appeared to have regained some whiteness since she'd quit a few years ago, but Luke also noticed some that were a little too white – false, he guessed, or capped. Other than that, she was the same as he had always remembered her. "You look good, boy," Billie said, finishing her appraisal. "City life must be doing right by you." She turned to lead him into the house.

"I have to look good," Luke replied with a smirk. "I have a beautiful wife to keep." Instantly he regretted the words; they seemed insensitive to say to a woman who had just lost her husband and was planning on leaving him anyway if he hadn't died. "Sorry," he said. "I didn't think about-"

Billie led Luke down the hall into the living room, waving her hand in the air to dismiss his apology. "Don't you worry 'bout it," she said, stepping into the cluttered living room. "I'm just glad *somebody* has a marriage that's workin' out. Lord knows, ain't none of my kids done it yet." Billie settled into an overstuffed recliner near the entrance and gestured towards a plastic-covered couch. "Go on, have a seat. Tell me what's goin' on with you."

Obediently, Luke moved towards the couch and paused to clear some books and pictures out of the way before sitting down. "Well ... things are good out in Seattle. I just got promoted to assistant manager, and Sierra's bookstore is going good."

"That's good, that's good," Billie said, nodding. Books, papers, pictures and scrapbooks filled most of the room around them; the only clear spots seemed to be a table besides Billie's chair and the area around the large, old TV in the corner of the room opposite Luke and Billie. The coffee table in front of Luke was also cluttered with pictures, most of them black-and-white. She gestured at the plastic bag in Luke's hand. "So what you brung me?"

"Oh," Luke said, looking at the bag as though it had suddenly materialized in his hand. "This is James' stuff. His clothes, wallet, stuff like that. Tim gave it to me."

Billie gave a derisive snort and settled back in her chair. "You can keep that shit. Or toss it on the curb for trash day tomorrow. That's where Chris is puttin' the rest of his shit, when he gets up."

"Oh, Chris is here?"

"Yeah, he's sleepin' right now, he worked all night at the Nissan plant. He'll be gettin' up soon." Billie took a drink from a faded plastic cup beside her, then looked at Luke with her head tilted. "You talked to Tim?"

Luke sighed. "Yeah, I did. I'm making the funeral arrangements for James, which is what I'm here about."

"I ain't doin' it," Billie said, jutting out her chin. "That sonofabitch cheated on me 3 times in six years of bein' married. Or, I should say, had three *affairs* in six years of marriage. He can burn in Hell for all I care."

"Billie. . ." Luke hated the pleading tone in his voice.

"He brought one of them *here*, Luke. One of the nurses from his chemo sessions, he brought that ho *here*. To *my house*." Billie pointed at the floor, then to her right. "In *my bed*. While I was workin' my ass off, he was here, havin' his way with his *chemo* nurse."

"Billie. . ."

"Don't you 'Billie' me, Luke. I said 'no' when the hospital called, and I'm sayin' 'no' to whatever you want, too." She crossed her arms as she spat out the words.

"Billie, his funeral is going to cost eight thousand dollars. I can't afford to pay for it by myself."

"Luke, I'm truly sorry you got stuck takin' care of that sorry sumbitch. But you shoulda did like I did and hung up when the hospital called you."

"Because you're mad at him, you're going to throw all his stuff out on the street and not help me put him to rest, finally?" Luke said, his temper rising as hers did.

"Because he disrespected me and my house, Luke. Don't you see that?"

"I have to ask myself," Luke said, struggling to contain the words but knowing it was too late, "how you didn't see that coming, seeing as while he was fucking you and gave you two children, he was also fucking my mother and gave her *three* children, *and* gave his *actual wife* three children. Fuck's sake, Billie, he left out of living with my mother to come marry *you*. How did you not see his infidelity coming a country fucking mile away?"

"Because I *loved* him!" Billie yelled, her eyes suddenly wet, the force of her outburst making Luke lean back on the sofa. The old plastic covering crinkled and cracked beneath him. "Because I loved that man, and I thought . . . maybe he would really do it, maybe he would really change this time." She wiped a tear away from her cheek. "I really did, and maybe I'm a fool for that, but I did. And he is gone now, and I ain't wastin' no more of my life on him. No money, no time, no nothin'. James Jackson put one wife in the grave over his bullshit – pardon my French – and I ain't lettin' him worry me into mine."

It hadn't been Luke's plan to make a widow cry today, but here he was, and there she was, softly sobbing into her hands. Way to go, jackass, Luke thought, staring at the plastic bag in his lap to avoid Billie's eyes.

"And you shouldn't talk to me like that in my own house," Billie said, regaining her composure abruptly.

"You're right," Luke mumbled. "I'm sorry, Billie."

Billie pulled a handkerchief from a dress pocket, blew her nose into it, and put it back. "Alright then. Just don't be as sorry as yo' daddy was."

Luke kept looking at the plastic bag, not looking up until he felt Billie's hand land on his forearm and squeeze it softly. His own wet eyes looked up into hers, which had silvery tear trails leading down from them.

"Luke, you might have loved your daddy, but he was a piece of shit through and through, pardon my language. Whyever you came back to bury him, you shouldn't have. You shoulda forgot about him and moved the hell on with your life."

Luke had no answer for that. Before he could come up with one, a voice came from the hallway behind him.

"Mama! What you yellin' about?" Luke recognized the voice of Christopher, his half-brother.

"I'm just talkin' wit' Luke!" Billie bellowed back.

"Luke who?"

"Yo' brother Luke!"

"I'll be out in a minute!" Luke heard springs creaking as, he assumed, Christopher climbed out of bed, then the sounds of shuffling and getting dressed.

"Luke," Billie said softly, pulling his attention back to her. "I got this out, was gonna give it to whoever handled James' funeral." She handed him a green plastic shopping bag. Luke looked inside and saw a folded grey suit. "It's James', it was the only one he had. Take that to Tim. That's all I'm gon' do, though. That stuff in the bag you brought, that's yours too. You keep it. You know you meant more to him than any of us did."

"That's not –"

"Yeah it is, you know it is. But when it's done, when he's dead and gone, you get away from here and you come back as little as possible, you heard me? That's what he –"

"BRUTHA-MAN!"

Luke and Billie both turned towards the booming voice. Christopher emerged from the hallway, his arms wide as he entered the living room. Luke stood up, struggling to hide his surprise: like his full brother, his half-brother had changed dramatically.

He knew why; Constance had told him when Christopher was diagnosed as diabetic, but he hadn't seen his brother since then. Luke still remembered him as being burly, more muscular, more youthful; not as this milk-chocolate-skinned gaunt scarecrow that finally looked the ten years older than Luke that he really was. More surprising to Luke than the strength of the hug was how strong it *wasn't*. "Heyyyy, Chris," Luke said, embracing his half-brother gingerly.

"Wassup, little brother? Not that much littler anymore," Chris said, playfully punching at Luke's belly.

"Nothing much," Luke replied, half-heartedly deflecting the punches. "What's up with you?"

"Aw, same ol', same ol'. You and Mama done talkin'?"

"Yeah," Luke said, looking at Billie and still finding sadness in her eyes. Sadness, and no help for his problem.

"Come outside with me then," Chris said. "It looks nice out and I need some fresh air."

Luke looked to Billie as she stood up from her chair, but she waved them off. "Y'all go on outside. I'm old, I need a nap. And *you*, Christopher, need to quit smokin'."

"I know, Mama, I know, I will. But not today," Chris replied, holding the screen door open as Luke gave Billie a farewell hug.

"Don't you bother him about that funeral," Billie whispered as they hugged. "He got problems of his own right now, you hear me?"

"Yes, ma'am," Luke whispered back and let her go. Thinking the conversation over, he caught the door that Christopher held open for him. Before he could step through, Billie spoke again.

"Good seeing you again, Luke! Come see me again before you leave town, okay?"

"Will do, Billie," Luke said, gently closing the screen door behind him. Christopher had taken a seat on the porch in an old wooden chair and was pulling another one to his side. Looking down at him, Luke was suddenly saddened by the way Chris's blue polo shirt hung on his thin frame. His tan slacks seemed like windsocks on his newly spindly legs. Even, to Luke's dismay, Chris's worn, brown loafers looked oversized, below his sagging white socks. *At least his voice is still the same.* "Wearing blue out here, bro? You lookin' to get shot?"

"Nah, man, Riverton ain't like that no more, least not over here. Cigarette?" Chris said, pulling a crumpled pack of Dorals and a lighter from his pocket.

"Brought my own," Luke replied, reaching down to the lower pocket on his cargo pants and pulling out a pack of cloves and a Zippo.

"I forgot, you like them *fancy* cigarettes," Chris teased, a smile on his face. That smile reminded Luke of his – their – father. "Whatcha call those, again?

Luke lit his cigarette, then his brother's. "Cloves," he replied. "I can't handle normal cigarettes. Ain't you supposed to have quit when you turned diabetic?"

Chris waved a hand in the air. "I was *supposed* to quit a lot of things, and I did most of 'em. Some habits are harder to let go of than others, ya know? Anyway, man, the east side of Riverton is doin' good, gettin' better. No more of those drugs and gang stuff over here. West side, though, that's still pretty rough."

"Huh. I guess this place *can* change."

"Yeah, it can. I ain't takin' credit for it, but you know I'm the youth deacon now over at Mt. Olive. We been getting a lot of the gangstas in, comin' lookin' for the Lord. That street stuff gets old after a while."

"I'll take your word for it. It was never my style."

"Far as I know, it wasn't, but you always looked like you was up to *somethin'*." Chris laughed. His laugh, too, reminded Luke of their father. "What's goin' on in Seattle? How you doin'? How's your wife? I ain't seen her since the wedding."

"We're all right. I'm assistant manager at the restaurant now, and her bookstore is doing good." Luke smiled weakly, not wanting to seem like he was bragging. Luke repeated the basic facts that he'd said already to so many people, but felt a twinge of guilt as he looked at his brother. Somehow, it felt like bragging when he said it to Christopher. It had felt more like a challenge to Constance, and only Billie had seemed okay with what he had to say.

"So you came back for the funeral, huh?"

"Yeah." But Luke couldn't help wondering, even if he dug up the money for the funeral, whether anyone would attend. Christopher might, but nobody else he'd already spoken to would. He wondered again if coming here had been a waste of time and money. According to everyone he'd talked to so far, it certainly was..

"You mighta wasted your time, little bro," Chris said, then took a deep drag of his cigarette. "Don't nobody wanna take care of him. I talked to Phoebe and them, and they don't want no part of dealin' with him." Phoebe was the youngest of their shared half-sisters; she and her sisters, Alexis and Danette, were James' children by his first wife. Danette was long gone from Riverton, and Luke doubted Phoebe would want to help, but he still had hope for Alexis.

"Yeah," Luke said, letting his shoulders slump, "I kinda figured that would be the case."

"I did my part," Chris said, lighting another cigarette. "I ran outside when I heard the ambulance comin', and I was in the ambulance with him when he died, 'cause Momma decided to follow us in her car. And you know what?"

"What?" Luke asked, fearful of the answer.

"Even on his deathbed, even as he knew he was dyin', that bastard *still* wouldn't tell me he loved me. That's all I ever wanted from him, just those three words, just some sign that I mattered to him. That's all I wanted. And even on his damn deathbed, he still wouldn't say it. Just muttered and mumbled his way right into Hell. I was so pissed off, I walked out when we got to the hospital, got in Momma's car, tol' her what happened, and sat in the car 'till she was ready to go. Do you know what that's like?"

Luke took a heavy drag of his clove, his mind running through all the things he'd never heard from his parents, like expressions of pride or love. "Yeah."

"Did he ever tell you that?"

"What? No, no. I don't remember him telling me that." Luke skimmed his memories. "No, I don't think he ever did."

"Not even after you saved his life?"

Luke turned to see a somewhat smug smile on Chris's face, the smile of someone who knows a secret. "You're not supposed to know about that," Luke said, lighting a second clove.

"You expected Rebekah to keep a secret?" Chris laughed, coughed, laughed again. "How long you known your sister, bro?"

"Fair point," Luke said.

"I wondered for a long time how he suddenly ended up livin' with Phoebe, but you know me, I don't like to pry. Rebekah told me about it a few years later. That was what, ten years ago?"

"Eleven this Christmas," Luke replied softly. He didn't like thinking about that night, about the hands around his father's neck, the fight he couldn't win against the enraged man determined to kill James, and the solution ... the only one he had been able to think of.

"Maybe that's why you were his favorite," Chris said, breaking into Luke's regretful recollection. "Maybe he knew you were the only one that would ever try to save him when the devil came to collect his due."

"I don't think that was it," Luke admitted. He'd never had any idea why he had been the "favorite," but he was sure as hell sick of hearing about it. It ruined any pleasure he might have had when James did deign to act like a father towards him.

"You don't, huh? Guess it'd be unlikely for him to see that far ahead. He wasn't exactly known for thinkin' past his next piece of ass."

"True dat," Luke replied, and looked out over the neighborhood, not wanting to talk about James anymore. The other houses on both side of the block looked much the same as Billie's: simple houses with simple porches, built in the post-World War II boom in Riverton to house all the incoming workers for US Gypsum, Boeing, and others. But those companies had left for greener pastures back in the 1970s, and left the houses behind for wealthy families to snatch up and rent to the economically devastated Rivertonians. The neighborhood had been rough in his youth; looking at it now, Luke had to admit that it was nicer now. Kids were actually playing outdoors (still mostly black, but he was a little surprised to notice some Hispanic children riding bikes as well), and people weren't ducking for cover every time a slow-moving vehicle rolled down the street.

"So, he never told you he loved you, either?" Chris asked.

"Nope," Luke said, hoping the short answer would end the talk of James, so that they could move on to better topics.

"See, you're wrong," Chris said, leaning towards Luke. "I think he did. Just not with words."

"How so?"

"When he had to leave town after Letitia died, you were the only one he kept in touch with. You were the only one he sent money to. I think that was the way he said 'I love you,' with money, instead of words."

"Huh," Luke replied, noncommittally. He had often wondered the same thing, but wanted the conversation to move on. He *knew* James' crimes against his children, had replayed them over and over again many times in his head. He couldn't fix them, though, and Chris's words were like festering sores that Luke could not heal. "So-," he began.

"Hang on, Luke," Christopher interrupted. "If you look at it that way, he told you, over and over again." Chris stubbed out his cigarette as clouds crossed his sunken cheeks. "Sumbitch never told me, not even on his deathbed."

"And here I thought forgiveness was a primary tenet of Christianity."

"Like I said, little bro, some things are harder to do than others."

"He left living with my mother to come here," Luke said, trying to sound positive. "That has to count for something."

"He came here because your grandma tried to shoot him." Chris said. "Didn't know that, did you?"

Luke definitely didn't want to talk about that, so he tried to change the subject again. "How are your girls doing?"

"They're good, they're good," Chris replied, smiling proudly. "Keisha got a science award last year. . ."

****

Luke walked to his car, both plastic bags in his hand. *Well, at least I've got the suit now.* As he got in, he tossed the plastic bags onto the passenger seat; James' wallet fell out of the bag of effects and onto the floor. Luke reached for it, to put it back in the bag, but once it was in his hand, he paused. He didn't even know basic facts about his father. Thinking about it, he realized that the wallet would tell him a great deal about the man who couldn't be bothered to do the same while he was alive.

There were no pictures of anyone in the middle, like most people would have. The wallet was surprisingly bare, containing only a debit card, a driver's license, and, to Luke's sarcastic amazement, no condoms. All that was in the cash section was a beat-up picture. Luke pulled it out and looked at it; it was so worn that it was hard to make out at first, but then he realized what it was.

It was Luke and Sierra at their wedding, five years ago. They were at the altar, kissing after saying "I do". Though the picture was very faded and worn, he could clearly make out their faces and some details of their clothing. But a picture so new would only have gotten that worn that fast if it had been handled a lot, if it had gotten fingerprint oils and sunlight on it a lot, when not being held in a closed, damp wallet.

Luke felt angry tears pricking his eyes as he put the picture back into the wallet. No pictures of Christopher or his kids, Rebekah or her kids, none of his wives or mistresses, nothing and no one else but him. Like the others were not worth remembering. Before putting the wallet back into the bag, he glanced at the driver's license.

"Huh," he said to no one, "so *that's* his birthday."

****

"I stopped at Captain D's," Luke said, stepping into Constance's kitchen with plastic bags in hand.

"Well that was nice of you, Luke, but you didn't have to do that," Constance replied, though she beamed at seeing the bags.

"I didn't do it *just* for you," Luke said, smiling, as he set the bags on the dining room table. Constance went into the kitchen to get plates while Luke set out boxes of fried fish fillets and containers of hush puppies, mashed potatoes, and gravy. "They don't have Captain D's in Seattle, so I haven't had any in a long time."

"I figured." Constance opened a box and took out three pieces of fish, putting them on a plate with mashed potatoes and a hush puppy.

"I brought enough for Matthew and Rebekah, too," Luke said. He sat down across the table from his mother, his plate loaded with fish, hush puppies, and several small packets of malt vinegar.

He sprinkled the vinegar over the fried fillets while Constance talked. "Matthew will eat later, and Rebekah's taking a nap. How did the arrangements go?"

Luke quickly swallowed the bite of fish in his mouth. "It didn't go too good," he said. "It's going to cost $8,000 for everything."

"Eight thousand dollars? My goodness!" Constance said, sounding shocked. "I don't think James had that much money left."

"He didn't have *any* money left. I've been trying to raise it, but Billie says she can't contribute, Christopher's broke, and Phoebe, Danette, and Alexis - well, I'm pretty sure you know how they feel."

Constance laughed. "Yeah, I reckon so. So who's going to pay for it?"

Luke turned his attention to the hush puppies on his plate and took a bite out of one. "I claimed his body, Mother," he answered between chews. "I have to pay for it somehow."

"Oh, Luke, I knew you should have never got involved. You don't have that kind of money sittin' around, do you?"

Constance was the patron saint of Not Getting Involved. Luke remembered her Not Getting Involved when he was being bullied, when he fought with his brother. She didn't Get Involved when Luke's dog was shot by hunters, and told him Not to Get Involved when he tried to help other people. He bit back anger, knowing that it would be useless at best, and giving her exactly what she wanted at worst. "No, I don't. At most, I could cover five thousand. And that's only if I can get Sierra to go along with it."

"Well, don't look at me. We got to fix up the church, and I need to get a new well dug. I can't do anything right now. You shoulda never got involved."

"Mother, we're past that. Nobody else would do anything."

"Well, you shoulda let that go."

With a trembling hand, Luke put down the piece of fish he was holding. "It is the saddest thing in the world to me, Mother, to think of someone – *anybody* – being so unwanted and unwelcome in life that he can't even get a decent funeral after his death." If Constance noticed the angry tone in his voice, she gave no sign of it. Luke cleared his throat to help get his voice under control and continued. "It's sad to me to think of anybody being that alone and that unloved. Bad enough to feel that way –" *when I was little,* Luke wanted to add, but stopped himself before the words came out. A fight with Constance would not help his cause.

Constance looked away, a certain hurt in her dark, suddenly wet, eyes. "Well … I can't help. I can't do it."

"I didn't come to ask for money anyway," Luke said. Had he actually managed to hurt her feelings? That idea came as a shock. Perhaps this was just a guilt-inducing feint? Whatever the case, he'd have to deal with it later; for now, he had business to take care of.

"What do you want, then?"

"If I can have the funeral at Gethsemane, that'll save on the church fees. If you ask Reverend July, I'm sure he'll do it for free; he's been a friend of the family long enough. After that, if I bury James in the family cemetery, I can dig the grave myself and save on that, too. I think that'll take the price down low enough that I can afford to do it, though it'll mean Sierra and I probably won't get a vacation this year." It would mean more than that, and Luke knew it. Telling Constance so would only renew her "never get involved" battle cry, however, so he understated the financial impact.

Constance stared at her lap. "I don't know, Luke," she muttered. "He wasn't a Washington, you know, he wasn't one of us."

"He helped create three of us; that should count for something."

"Luke," she said, finally raising her head to meet his eyes, "that man hurt everybody he ever met. He started Tim drinkin', did you know that? And he killed Letitia-"

"Letitia committed suicide; why does everyone seem to forget that? Her choice, not his."

"He might as well have pushed her off that bridge, the way he humiliated her."

With your help, Luke thought, but bit back the words. "I promise you, Mother, I've heard enough today about James' crimes." His voice made the quotes around the final word apparent. "But at the end of the day, he's gotta go somewhere, and somebody has to pay for it."

"Why not just let the county cremate him?" That now-familiar refrain – let the county handle it. Everybody had asked that question: Constance, Billie, Chris, and now Constance again. It was simple to Luke, much like he felt it would have been simple to his grandmother; whatever else James had been in life, he was a problem for the family to handle, not complete strangers. It would not have felt right to Luke to hand James over, even though he resented his father. Why didn't anyone else seem to understand that?

"He wouldn't have wanted that, and I didn't want him sitting forgotten on a shelf somewhere." Below the table, Luke flexed the fingers of his left hand: open, closed, open, closed. "Because *somebody* had to. He was *family*. It's your fault he was family, but he was, in the end, *family*."

Constance didn't reply. She stood, took her plate, and gave Luke an inscrutable glare before walking into the kitchen. Behind her, the kitchen door suddenly swung open,

Bingo's bark heralding the entrance of the man who stepped through.

"Hey there," Werner said, a radiant smile on his face.

"Hey," Luke replied, looking at his half-full plate. He could feel Werner's eyes on him.

Werner stared at Luke for a second, then looked at Constance, who stood at the kitchen sink, her back still turned. His smile faltered. "What's going on here?"

"Nothin'," Constance muttered.

"I'm trying to talk her into letting me bury James in the family cemetery and use the church for the funeral," Luke said.

"Why?" Werner said, standing at the table with his arms crossed.

Luke sighed. "Because if I don't, it'll cost eight thousand dollars, and I can't afford that. If I do, I think it'll take about five thousand, which I can pay but I'll be tight for a while."

"Huh," Werner said thoughtfully. "Luke, I brought some gas for the tractors and some lumber for fixin' the roof next week. Why don't you go get those outta the truck? I'll be out in a minute."

The request made Luke feel twelve years old again, forced to leave the room while the adults talked. He wanted to insist upon staying, but Werner's pose and tone told him that arguing wouldn't help. He got up from the table and went outside without a word.

As he lifted a load of lumber, Luke thought back over the conversation with Constance. Had she really hated James so much that she wouldn't let him be buried in the cemetery? She must have loved him, in some form or fashion, despite how he had treated his children and their mothers, so was it so hard to help out?

But that, of course, required Getting Involved, even in such a miniscule way as granting permission. Did she fear that Billie and the others would hate *her* for it? Just for saying yes to his idea to save money? Or was there something else going on that he just didn't know? That was always the problem with Constance – you never quite knew where you stood, except in knowing that blowing up at her was, for her, a win. Every conversation with her about anything serious felt like a fight you couldn't win because you didn't know the rules-

The door to the kitchen closed, bringing Luke out of his thoughts. He turned with the last load of lumber in his arms to see Werner standing in the garage.

"Well?" Luke asked, setting the lumber in its place.

"You can use the church and the cemetery, but you're on your own for digging the grave and filling it in. I'll talk to Reverend July and make sure he's there."

Luke breathed a sigh of relief. "Thanks, Uncle Werner. You're the first person that's been willing to help me all day."

Werner put his hand on Luke's shoulder. "Don't be too harsh on yo' momma, son. James hurt her a lot. Your brother and sister, too."

"But not me, right? Just because he gave me money –" Luke couldn't help thinking of the conversation with Chris, that the money was never just money, it was attention and love and everything James never gave his other children – "that makes everything okay?" The bitterness in Luke's voice made him feel even more like a twelve-year-old; he hated it, but couldn't drop it. "The money didn't make school or growing up any easier. I mean, you and the other uncles helped, but nobody taught me how to talk to girls or –"

"I've seen Sierra; I think you did pretty goddamn good on your own," Werner said with a grin. Luke couldn't help smiling back, feeling his anger subside as he did. "Look, you should probably get on back to town. Constance ain't feelin' very talky right now."

"Oh wait, I wanted to ask her about something Chris said . . ."

Werner put his hand on Luke's shoulder. "Ask later."

"I guess it can wait—oh bloody hell," Luke said, looking at his watch. "It's already 4. I need to get back to Tim before 6."

"Go do that, then."

"I will." Luke fished the rental car keys out of his pocket. He stuck out his hand to Werner. "Thanks, Uncle Werner."

"Ain't no thang. Good luck."

"Good luck with what?"

"Talkin' Sierra into spendin' the money."

****

"I'm really sorry about this," Luke said, shifting his grip on the phone so he could close the car door behind him.

"Can we really afford it, though?" Sierra replied. "We really need to get the furnace done before winter, and my car is still making that weird noise-"

"I'll see if Andrew or Josh can take a look at the car when I get back – at least then we'll only have to pay for parts. And I can ask Paul about getting some overtime in." Luke paused outside the glass doors of the funeral home to finish the call. "I'm pretty sure we can cover it, with a little financial creativity and calling in some favors."

Sierra sighed. "I know you need this, Luke. We'll make it work – but you better be happy you're so damn cute. I miss you."

"I miss you too. This trip has been really rough. I wish you could have come with me—" Luke heard someone calling for Sierra in the background.

"I need to go," she said. "Trina's got a problem. Love you, baby."

"Love you too, Sierra," Luke said, before he pressed the "end call" button. He wasn't sure if she'd heard him, she'd had to hang up so quickly, but he felt better for having said it.

When he looked up at the glass doors, Tim was standing on the other side, face against the glass, red-rimmed eyes wide and staring at him. Luke yelled, startled.

"Oh shit, that was funny," Tim laughed as he opened the door. A slight whiff of alcohol exited as Luke entered.

"You coulda given me a fucking heart attack, jackass!"

"At least they wouldn't have had to move you far," Tim laughed, leading Luke towards the office. "Gimme a break, it's a funeral home. We don't get many laughs around here. So what's up? We gonna do this?"

"Yeah," Luke replied, calming down. "Gotta make some adjustments to the plan, though."

Pandem Buckner

CHAPTER FOUR

Luke awoke Friday morning in a surly mood.

It stayed with him as he crawled out of bed and dropped the floor for his morning push-ups. His mood stayed surly and grumpy as he did some jumping jacks and crunches, and then it followed him into the shower. It clung to him while he washed his hair, lived in his mind as he brushed his teeth, and didn't go anywhere as he dressed for the day in a purple t-shirt and black jeans.

Dressed and ready, he sipped a bottle of juice from room's mini-fridge, though the expense of it only added to his surliness, and considered all he had to do that day.

After yesterday's events, he didn't feel like dealing with Chris or Billie again. Constance already knew; he'd have her call and tell Billie when the wake and funeral would be if she hadn't already. Rebekah and Matthew knew, since Constance did. Of James' children, that left only Alexis, since Danette was out of town. And Phoebe.

Danette had moved out of town a few years after her mother's death and never returned, so he would have to trust Alexis would get word to her, if she even cared. Luke smiled a little; of all his half-siblings, Alexis was far and away the easiest to deal with. She was always pleasant to him and seemed to bear little resentment over her mother's death and their father's favoritism. Maybe there was something to being a Jehovah's Witness; Alexis was always calm and reasonable, so it was clearly working for her. That part of the day would be enjoyable, at least. But Phoebe. . .

Phoebe had always hated him, from the start. He never knew exactly why; perhaps it was because they were the closest in age, or maybe that he'd been James' favorite. Luke didn't know and didn't really care; he only knew that she had always been nasty towards him, and he had always been nasty right back to her on the few occasions they'd been forced to share space. When he had taken their father to live with her, the morning after The Incident with Matthew, she hadn't said a single word to Luke, only gestured at him to leave the boxes at the door.

Visiting Phoebe would indeed be the day's bitterest pill, harder even than the hours he'd spend digging a grave afterwards. The wake was scheduled for Saturday evening, necessitating grave preparation the day before so that he wouldn't show up to the wake sweaty and tired. Then the funeral Sunday, and after that he could finally get on a plane and go back to Seattle. He was already tired of this place and its depressing atmosphere of constant struggle. In case he'd forgotten that for a few minutes, the hotel parking lot provided an example. As he opened the door and saw two homeless people, both too dirty and bedraggled to make out their gender, arguing while digging through the trash dumpster. The feeling that dominated his youth, that he needed to get out of this place and never come back, returned to him suddenly, familiar and strong.

Phoebe, Luke thought, opening the door of the rental car. *Might as well get it over with.* As he drove off, he had the thought that maybe his surly mood was just his mind preparing for dealing with Phoebe.

****

Phoebe lived in the northwestern part of Riverton, on the edge between the shopping-heavy affluence of the north end and the gang-ridden poverty of the west. Though some of the neighborhoods he drove through to reach her townhouse made him nervous, her complex looked nice enough. The sameness of the beige townhouses and the security gate around the property made it feel a bit more secure, even though he noticed a car nearby with a missing window and glass shards sprinkled on the ground as he parked. He made sure to park as close to her townhouse as he could, and triple-checked that the car alarm was set before knocking on her door.

"Who is it?" a slightly slurred voice asked from behind the door. Luke checked his phone; it was only 11 AM. Had she already been drinking?

"It's your brother," Luke replied. He heard a chain unlatch, then the door swung open to reveal his half-sibling.

Phoebe stood about 5'5", with a curvy figure, which was not uncommon to the populace of Riverton. Her hazel-brown eyes were rimmed with red; she had clearly been either drinking or crying, perhaps both, but neither the eyes nor the early drinking were what made Phoebe different. Her nasty attitude was also not that unusual in Riverton. Her hair, dyed dark blonde and somewhat trimmed at shoulder-length, was unusual, but not very much so. What truly set Phoebe apart, even from him, was her skin.

Several shades lighter than even his skin, Phoebe was so light in skin tone that she very nearly appeared to be an albino. This had earned her much gossip over whether or not she was truly James's daughter, especially since all of the other children were Luke's color or darker, and her full sister Alexis was very, very dark. However, James had never to Luke's knowledge contested or denied Phoebe's parentage, and Letitia had never confessed to any sort of infidelity before her death. Moreover, she, Luke, and Matthew were the only three of James' children who had freckles. Luke felt that should have tied them together, but instead seemed to drive them further apart.

"Oh, it's *you*," Phoebe said, sneering in disgust. "I thought it was Chris." Dressed in knee-length jean shorts and a loose t-shirt, she looked exactly as Luke remembered her. Unlike almost everyone he'd visited so far, neither time, illness, or raging alcoholism seemed to have had any real effect on Phoebe.

"Why, does your soul need saving? He's gonna need a lot of Bibles for that one." Luke smiled, hoping the joke would break the ancient tension between them.

Phoebe sneered even harder. "What the hell do you want?"

"If you're not busy, I think we need to talk. Please."

Phoebe sighed, then leaned out of the door to look up and down the row of houses. "All right, get in here before the neighbors think I lowered my standards."

They'd be more surprised to know that you had standards, Luke thought, but kept the words to himself as he stepped through the door and closing it softly behind him. The inside of the house was as bland as the outside: beige walls dominated. He followed Phoebe into the living room. Above the sofa hung a large framed picture of a beautiful, caramel-skinned woman with almond-shaped eyes, a pert, cute nose, and a wide, dazzling smile. *Letitia*, Luke thought, *frozen in beauty forever*. He moved a couple of the magazines out of his way and took a seat on end of the sofa closest to the door. Phoebe plopped down on the other end.

"How have you been?" Luke asked, hoping that pleasantries would make this conversation different. "We haven't talked in-"

"What do you want?" Phoebe interrupted, lifting a glass of amber liquid from the table. "If you came to tell me Daddy is dead, I already know that."

I'm doing good, thanks, how are you? Luke chided himself for the sarcastic thought. He really wanted this time to be different, even if she didn't care enough to ask how he'd been. "I know. Chris told me yesterday."

"And I know you didn't come to ask for money, because I ain't givin' a dime to help that fucker."

"Chris told me that, too. That's already taken care of." Luke felt another feeling settle into him: regret. He hated that time and death had changed nothing between them, that they were always going to be at each other's throats and he had no idea why. He resolved to keep his words calm and sweet, to try to keep things nice between them for once.

"You shouldn't have either. But I knew you would, because you always were the golden boy. The good child.

The *favorite*." To Luke's ears, Phoebe said "favorite" with the same tone and inflection that most people used to say "herpes."

"Somebody had to, Phoebe; it might as well have been me."

"Nobody *had* to. You shoulda just let his ass rot." She took another sip from her glass. "Done is done, though. So if that's all taken care of, what do you want?"

"I just came to let you know that the wake is tomorrow night. It's at Kirkman. The funeral is going to be Sunday at Gethsemane, in case you care to attend."

"I don't," Phoebe replied, taking a cigarette out of a pack on the table and lighting it. "You couldn't have called and told me that?"

"Your father is dead; I'm telling you about his funeral. I felt you deserved something more personal than a phone call."

"The good son," Phoebe said, sneering at him again as she took a drag of her cigarette. "The thoughtful, kind one."

"Look, I'm just trying to do the right thing here, Phoebe," Luke said, hoping that the exasperation he felt didn't creep into his voice. "When somebody dies, arrangements have to be made, things have to be taken care of. *I* did that. All I'm doing is letting you know when the funeral is, in case you want to go." *To make sure he's dead, if nothing else.*

"I really don't, though." She took another drink. "Are you asking me to go?"

"I think it'd be good for you to go. It might help you get closure. After all, no matter what, he was your father."

Phoebe made a dismissive gesture with her unoccupied hand. "For all that's worth. Yeah, he helped create me, but that's about all. Even when Momma was alive, he was too busy with 'work' to make time for me." Her hand was unsteady as she set the glass down. "Too busy fuckin' his little skanks, more like."

"Phoebe, he wasn't around for me, either. Even less so after what happened with Letitia—"

"Don't you talk about my momma," Phoebe said, her voice growing angry. "She was a *lady*. She carried herself well, she took good care of herself and her kids, she was a loving and faithful wife to that motherfucker. He couldn't walk a block without fallin' into some ass. Fuck him." She shook her glass; ice cubes rattled in the bottom. "I'm getting some more," she said, standing up. "You want some?"

"It's a little early for me, thanks," Luke answered, blowing out a deep sigh as she stepped into the kitchen. He strongly considered leaving as he listened to the clinking glass and sloshing liquid of Phoebe making herself another drink. Before he could stand, Phoebe returned to her seat, lighting a new cigarette with the burning butt of the first. She tossed the old one into an ashtray and took a heavy gulp of whiskey before turning to him again.

"Why did you come back?"

The question caught Luke off-guard. "I had to. Nobody else, and I mean nobody, was willing to even handle his funeral arrangements. What else was I supposed to do? I would have had to come back for the funeral anyway."

"Why?"

Luke raised his eyebrow. "What do you mean, why?"

"Why would you be even that loyal to somebody who wasn't there for you, as you said? Why would you bother doing anything nice for somebody like that? For somebody who left your mother, cheated on both of his wives, and killed my mother?"

"I don't ..." Luke stumbled for words and found himself coming up blank. "It was ... somebody had to take care of it, I mean. I don't know what you're looking for."

"I think you felt guilty." Her red-rimmed eyes focused on his; the intensity of her stare unnerved Luke. "You were his favorite and you hadn't talked to him in five years. You got more of his time and money than any of us did, yet you were the one that argued with him and stopped talkin' to him and ran off to the West Coast chasin' some white woman. I guess he'd have been proud of you for that, turning your back on him to go get some ass."

"Maybe he would have been proud of you for all the dick you went through in high school." Phoebe's eyes widened at that remark and Luke felt his own pulse race as the words came out. *Here we go ...* "We didn't go to the same school, but Riverton is a small, small town, Phoebe."

"And *I* heard you saved his worthless ass when somebody was trying to kill him. You should have let him die. Who was that? Oh, lemme think, wait, I remember, it was –"

"None of your fucking business," Luke replied, an angry heat in his voice. He could feel his face growing redder every second.

"None of *my* business? The motherfucker that killed my momma about to get his? Shit, I wish I'd been there! I would cheered, or at least stopped *you* from gettin' in the fuckin' way."

"Right," Luke said, standing up. "Well, good seein' you Phoebe. Except it completely wasn't."

"What did you expect? You came here expecting me to act like I missed that fucker? Wrong house, wrong person, wrong life. Fuck him, and I would say fuck you too, but I can't hate you for feeling affection towards that fucker." Phoebe's cigarette bobbled wildly in the air as she spoke and gestured. "I would too if he'd kept in contact with me and sent me money while he was gone. At least then I'd feel my affection was well paid for."

Luke stopped, standing at the end of the couch. "You think I came back just because he sent me money?"

"No," she replied, taking another drag. "I think you came back because you took his money and turned your back on him for a woman. It's ironic as hell, but in a way, that's what he deserved. You got a better revenge on Daddy than all of us ever did. You were his favorite, and he had to die without saying a word to you in, what, five years? Six? Good fuckin' job, Luke!"

"I'm out of here," he said, moving towards the door. He heard the sound of Phoebe getting up behind him.

"Good, get out, run away! I hope you and your ho-ass momma have a good time at the funeral!"

Luke stopped, standing in the middle of the hallway. "My what?" he said, his voice and body suddenly feeling very cold.

"What else could she be? She fucked a married man for 8 years of his marriage! Her and Billie and fuck knows who else! My mother was happily married, until they came and fucked it all up! They pushed her just like he did! So fuck them too!" Her words definitely had a heavier slur than they had when Luke had arrived. He noticed it, but didn't care anymore.

"So who do you blame for the way you turned out? Promiscuous, angry, unloving, and unlovable? Was that their fault too?"

"*Fuck you, Luke!*" Phoebe yelled, flipping him off from the entrance to the hallway. Whiskey sloshed out of her glass as she yelled and gestured. "They killed my momma! You don't know what that's like! You don't know what I been through!"

Luke placed his hand on the doorknob, wanting so much to walk away, but the words in his throat held him there, stopped his feet, would not let him leave until they'd burst free, and he lost the will to fight against them. "Letitia killed herself," he said softly. "She drove to the middle of the river bridge, got out of her car, and jumped. 150 feet straight down, into the Mississippi River. Nobody else was there.   Nobody pushed her, Phoebe, not Billie, not Constance, not James. Nobody."

The glass smashed into the wall near his head, whiskey spilling onto his shirt and face as it flew by. Luke felt small shards brush his anger-reddened face, but didn't move.

"Fuck you! They took her away from me! *They* made her the laughingstock of the whole goddamn city! *They* humiliated her and killed her! I was only *seven years old* and *they* took my momma away!" Luke looked at Phoebe. She stood in the middle of the hallway, arms by her side, fists balled up so tight her knuckles were even paler than normal, her bloodshot eyes wet and furious, her chest heaving with quick, angry breaths. *If this were a cartoon, there'd be steam coming out of her ears.*

"Phoebe," he said, his voice still cold as he turned back to the door. "Letitia took *herself* away.   James humiliated her, yes, there is no doubt about that, and I know she was crushed by how long he'd fooled her, by the kids he had by other women. But *she* decided that her humiliation and pain meant more to her than being alive to take care of her children, Phoebe. She chose to die rather than face gossip and shame so she could be here for her kids. *She* took *herself* away from you. Nobody else did that, Phoebe, nobody else made that choice for Letitia. Hate James and Constance and Billie for what they did, but if you want to hate someone for Letitia's death, blame Letitia because she's the one that did it."

Luke barely heard Phoebe move before he felt her fists thumping hard against his back. *"Get out, get out you motherfucker, get out of my house, get out of my life, fuck you fuck you fuck you!"* she shouted, punching his back furiously as he opened the door and stepped through. She didn't follow him outside; as soon as he was out of her range, he stopped on the sidewalk and looked back at her. He only got a quick glimpse before he had to dodge a thrown umbrella, but he could see the tears streaming furiously down her pale cheeks, see the anger and rage written in her screaming, contorted features. *"Fuckin' go away and don't ever come back!"* .

In the parking lot, an elderly black woman got out of her car, then turned to look at them. "What *the fuck* are *you* looking at?" Phoebe yelled at her. The old woman raised her eyebrows and hurriedly shuffled off towards a townhouse across the lot.

Luke kept walking towards the rental car, Phoebe screaming obscenities at him, telling him not to ever come back as he left. He felt the thump of an ashtray hitting his shoulder, but tried his best not to visibly react to it. As he got into the car, he turned back in time to see the door to Phoebe's townhouse slam shut, so hard that the ornamental door-knocker dropped onto the sidewalk.

Sitting in the car, Luke turned the key in the ignition, and reached for the gear shift in the center console, but his wobbling hand would not move the shift. Instead, Luke sighed, put his head on the steering wheel, and, for the first time in months, perhaps years, wept silently. He stayed there, weeping in anger at himself, at Phoebe, at James, at everyone in this fucked-up family, for nearly an hour.

No one disturbed him.

****

Luke knocked softly on the white-painted wooden door.

"Who is it?" answered a feminine voice. Somehow, like it always had, her voice made him think of chocolate.

"Atheist missionary!" he replied through the door.

"Atheist missionary?" she replied, confusion in her voice. "What do you want?"

"Nothing," Luke replied with a smile. He wasn't sure if the joke was meant more for her sake or his, but he knew he definitely needed a laugh.

"Oh ha ha ha," Alexis said, opening the door. "That must be what passes for funny out in. . ." The sentence trailed off as she saw him, her dark brown eyes taking in his face, their tone passing from amusement to concern.

Alexis was the tallest of James' children, standing just a hair under six feet tall. While also curvy, her measurements weren't as voluptuous as Phoebe's, though her belly was considerably more rounded. Her thick, coarse hair was dark, but not as dark as Rebekah's, which Luke always figured had to do with Native American ancestry on Constance's side, and nowhere near as light as Phoebe's dyed locks. Alexis also had skin the colour of very, very dark chocolate. To top it off, she was a very calm, pleasant, hospitable person, making her the complete opposite of her younger sister. After the disaster with Phoebe, Luke really needed that calm pleasantness.

"I know *that* look," Alexis said, reaching out and pulling Luke into a warm hug. "You went and talked to Phoebe, didn't you?"

"Yeah," Luke replied, his word muffled by Alexis's shoulder.

"I told you last night that was a bad idea, didn't I?"

"Yeah."

"I swear," she said, letting him go and pulling back into her apartment, "you are ev'ry bit as hardheaded as yo' brothers. Come on in."

Luke followed her into the living room. The apartment was small, nice but not as messy as Luke had expected. Some clothes were scattered about the couch and chair, though the beige carpet was clean and looked freshly vacuumed. Alexis continued into the kitchen, separated from the living room only by a waist-high wall with an opening on one end for access. At Alexis's gesture, Luke took a seat at the round four-seater table in the kitchen. He had barely settled into the seat when a glass of water was placed on the blue-and-white-checkered tablecloth in front of him.

"You probably need a drink," Alexis said, smoothing out her loose-fitting pink slacks, "but around here, that's all you get."

"Man, the customer service in this place sucks," Luke replied, taking a sip from the glass.

Alexis took a seat across from Luke, another glass of water in her hand. "So do the tips, really." Luke chuckled at her joke, then idly toyed with the glass, staring at it, hoping Alexis would not ask— "So what happened with Phoebe?" *Dammit.*

"She didn't want to go to the funeral."

"And?"

"She was drunk."

"And?"

"She talked about Letitia and how James had killed her, and my mother and Billie were just – I believe she said 'ho-ass women' – that might as well have pushed Letitia along with him."

"And you said?"

Luke sighed, propped his elbows on the table, and put his forehead on his palms. "You sure you wanna know? It was pretty bad."

He could feel Alexis staring at him, even without raising his eyes from the tablecloth. She paused a beat, then softly said, "Tell me, Luke."

"I … I told her that nobody killed Letitia but Letitia, that Letitia was the one that decided to jump off the bridge, who decided her pain and humiliation meant more to her than staying in the lives of her children."

From the sound of her voice, Luke could tell Alexis was shaking her head as she spoke. "Lord, Lord, Lord. And what did she do?"

"Threw a glass of whiskey at me."

"Hoo, she musta been *pissed*. She ain't one to waste good alcohol. What else?"

"She started screaming at me to get out of her house, threw an ashtray at me, and yelled at an old woman in the parking lot. I sat in the car for a while, trying to … calm down before I came over here."

"Yeah," Alexis said, "that's about what she said. 'Cept you left out that you sitting in your car for so long freaked her out. She thought you were gonna come back with a gun or somethin'."

Luke peeked out between his fingers, his cheeks red with remembered shame. "She called you?"

"Yep," Alexis replied, sipping from her glass of water. "Not long after you left. She was drunk and cryin' and scared you was comin' to kill her."

"If you already talked to her, why did you make me tell you all that?"

Alexis gently smacked his forehead with her palm. "'Cause I wanted to hear yo' side, dummy. Lord help you two. Y'all set each other off easier'n most people say 'hello' to each other."

Luke clenched his hands together on the table and stared at them. "I don't know why she gets under my skin so easily. I had hoped we could have a peaceful talk today, about the funeral and about James…"

"Naw, she can't do that. She can't see that far past her own pain."

Head tilted, Luke stared at Alexis. "What do you mean?"

"Luke, Phoebe was the baby of James' kids before you came along. You know – and don't you argue with me – the baby of the family is *always* the one that gets spoiled. That was her, at least for us, until you showed up. And then Momma died, and Daddy left town, and she didn't have a momma or a daddy anymore, 'cause her daddy was too busy takin' care of you."

"I always wondered if that was it - but you and Danette lost your mother and father too, and y'all ain't bitter about it."

"I was 13 when Momma died. Danette was 15. We had plenty of time with Momma. Not enough, you know, but plenty. Phoebe was only 8. She didn't get that time like we did."

"That's the difference? You and Alexis got more time with her?"

"We was mo' mature when it happened, we understood death better. Did you understand death when you was 7? Don't answer that; you probably did, with yo' little smart ass. I can't say Danette really handled it well, since she left town and never came back. And Phoebe — Phoebe just never got over it, and I don't think she ever will."

Luke felt himself coming back together, felt the rational, analytical parts of his mind returning full function after shutting down at Phoebe's house. "It's a child's anger carried into adulthood, I get that," he said. "But why take it out on me?"

"Shoot, Phoebe takes that out on *everybody*, you ain't special."

"Heh," Luke said, chuckling in spite of his dour mood. "You remember my cousin Miles?"

"Used to live down the road from ya'll? Yeah, I remember him."

"He met Phoebe a couple of times, and every time he'd tell me the same thing: 'Phoebe would be pretty hot if she wasn't such a raging bitch.'"

Alexis laughed, a warm, soothing, peaceful laugh that, like her voice, sounded like chocolate. Hearing it made Luke feel a lot better. "Oh shoot, I hear that so much I thought it was my name for a while."

Luke laughed at that, and felt the knot in his chest loosen up.

"But, you know," Alexis said, "you look more like him than anybody else does, you sound more like him, you got that same quick sense of humor he had."

"Umm, Matthew looks just like me, remember?"

"Matthew's taller than you, he used to be rounder, and he dropped his sense of humor on his way out yo' momma."

"Fair enough," Luke said, settling back into the chair, feeling fully relaxed again. "But that doesn't explain why you aren't angry and bitter, too."

Alexis sighed again. "I put all that ol' stuff behind me a long time ago, Luke. I forgave Daddy in my heart even though he didn't ask me to, and I forgave Momma, too. I think she just didn't know how to deal with it and did the only thing she could figure out to do to get away from the pain." Luke hung his head as regret over his words to Phoebe resurfaced. Alexis reached across the table and took his hand in hers. "I don't mean what you said to Phoebe wasn't maybe true. I don't know what Momma was thinking when she jumped. But that's what gives me comfort, that she just didn't know how to handle it, so that's what I choose to believe. That's what lets me forgive her.

"Everything you said to Phoebe, that's what *she* believes, deep down inside. That's what I think. That's really how she feels, deep inside, and she has - I don't know what I'm trying to say. It's like she has a perfect picture of Momma in her mind, you know? She didn't have time to see Momma as a person, just as her momma, her world. When you're 8, yo' momma is your whole world. Yours too, don't argue. Whatever you might think about her now, Constance was your world when you were that age. 'S why you went to school where she taught 'stead of where the rest of us went."

Luke wanted to argue but couldn't. He knew the truth of Alexis's calm words.

"She didn't just lose her momma, she lost her daddy at the same time; she lost her whole world. And her daddy that she loved so much, she had to live with the uncles that took us in talkin' trash about him all the time. He left town 'cause they threatened to kill him, you know that."

Luke thought back to his conversation with Chris, then further back to that Christmas Eve eleven years ago. "Lot of that going around," he muttered.

"What?"

"Nothin'. Keep going."

"I'm just sayin', don't judge her too harsh."

Luke's wet brown eyes connected with Alexis's warm brown eyes. "Do you think she'll ever change?"

"I don't know, Luke, I honestly don't know. I pray for her every night, you know, for her to stop drinkin' and smokin' and sleepin' 'round and all that but mostly... I pray for her to find some peace in her heart. She might change, but she ain't ready yet, and the Lord ain't ready to make her change yet."

There was nothing more to be said about Phoebe, so Luke switched to Danette. "Does Danette know James is dead?"

"Yeah, she knows, I called her right after Chris called me."

"Guess she's not coming to the funeral, huh?"

"Nope! She is happy off in Chicago with her husband and their babies and she ain't never comin' back here. She said it when she left, and she meant it. Oh, hol' on a minute." Alexis got up from the table and went to the oven. Luke heard it creak open, and watched as she lifted out a baking sheet.

"What's that?" Luke asked, though the scent told him what they were.

"I made some chocolate chip pecan cookies for y'all. Soon as they cool, I'll put 'em in a Tupperware for you to take to Rebekah and them."

"Well that was nice of you. I'm sure they'll be greatly enjoyed."

"Luke, I'm callin' Rebekah tonight to make sure they all got there."

"Spoilsport."

"That's what Richie calls me," she said, taking her seat again.

"Where is he?"

"His narrow butt better be at school," Alexis replied. "And before you ask, naw, I ain't comin' to the funeral."

Luke was crestfallen; it was starting to look like this funeral would be a party of one. "Why not? You said you forgave him."

"I did. That don't mean I want anything to do with him. I forgave him, I moved on. I said my goodbyes to him a long time ago, in spirit, at least. I got my peace with him; funerals are for people who ain't got that peace yet."

Luke nodded at that, acknowledging the truth of her words. "I think the word you're looking for is 'closure.'"

"Shut up, I ain't ask you to correct me," Alexis said, gently punching his shoulder. "By the way, shouldn't you be goin' to dig a hole?"

"I was waiting for the waitress to bring me more water," Luke replied with a grin.

****

Luke prided himself on only having eaten three cookies by the time he reached Framer's Point Road. *Not bad*, he thought, licking the crumbs from his lips. *Now I just have to get a shovel from the house, spend a few hours digging a hole, and then try to get anybody to actually come to the funeral.* There was still hope for Rebekah, or maybe Matthew. He couldn't say which task he thought would be the least onerous. As he approached the cemetery, however, a large lump at the northern end of the cemetery suggested that maybe one of his tasks had already been done for him.

At the cemetery, Luke pulled over. His eyes had been honest with him from a distance: there was indeed a pile of dirt at the northern end of the cemetery. Now that he was on its southern side, he could also see a shovel there, with a white piece of paper waving from its handle. Curious, he got out of the car and jogged over to see what it was.

The note read: *I didn't do it for him, I did it for you. When family needs help, you do what you can. W. P.S. Take the shovel back up to the house.*

For the first time since arriving, Luke didn't feel quite so alone in dealing with his father's death., This would likely be the only help he got, at least from Werner. Still, he felt better as he walked back to the car, shovel in hand, leaves crunching under his feet.

As he expected, Rebekah's car was not at the house. Unexpectedly, Constance's car was gone as well. He checked his watch; it was already 3 o'clock and his mother was generally home from whatever errands she had to run by then. *Where is she?* he wondered, stepping around the sleeping form of Bingo to let himself into the house. He left the shovel beside the door, the note crumpled in his pocket.

"Hello?" he called out as he walked into the kitchen. No one answered. He wondered for a second if Matthew was home, but realized he was in no mood for talking to his brother after the fracas with Phoebe earlier, and decided to leave Matthew alone, if he was even there. He remembered the food he'd brought yesterday; a quick check of the refrigerator revealed plenty of fish left. He grabbed a plate from the cabinet, then loaded it with fish and put it in the microwave.

As he sat down at the dining room table to eat, he heard a car pull up outside. It never failed, he thought: sit down to eat and people show up. When the door swung open, he looked up, expecting to see Constance. Instead, the short, solid form of his sister Rebekah came in.

"Hey, Luke!" Rebekah said, walking towards him swiftly, arms open, a purse dangling from her left hand. Luke stood up and went over to her, holding her in a tight embrace. She was his favorite full sibling, though given his history with Matthew, it wasn't exactly a close contest.

"Hey, Rebekah!" Luke said, grinning broadly. Though she had lost some weight since he'd last seen her, she was still quite solid in build. Her straightened black hair was held back in a ponytail, and like their mother, she wore glasses, though hers were smaller and suited her prominent cheekbones. Her dress was patterned in red and brown leaves, which matched the autumn landscape outside very well, and she wore low maroon heels well-matched to her dress. *She always was the most fashionable*, Luke thought, letting her go and returning to the table. "What are you doing home?"

"I always get off early on Fridays," she replied, setting her purse on the table and taking a seat next to him. "I usually got so many errands to run that it's just easier for me to always get it off. Momma told me you were here, but I been busy."

"I know, Miss Socialite," Luke said with a smile. "Speaking of, where is she?"

"She called me; she went to town with Matthew to do some shopping."

"Oh, okay."

"So I heard you didn't have a good day," she said with a sly grin on her lips, but warm concern in her eyes. Luke had seen that concern in her eyes before; it had been there when he was little and woke up from a nightmare.

He'd been seven years old at the time, and had just become aware that other homes had both parents there. With his father absent, his young mind had figured that it must have been because his father didn't want him, and things his mother had said recently, in an angry mood, made him feel unwanted by her as well. Those factors had contributed to his childish nightmare, in which he'd been taken away by an orphanage because neither of his parents wanted him. The orphanage car was pulling away from the house, only his grandmother and sister standing in the driveway waving goodbye to him, when he'd woken up cradled in Rebekah's arms. She'd held him tight, whispering "shhhhh, shhhh, it was just a bad dream" as he'd cried about the dream and tried to explain it between sobs. She'd held him until he finally went back to sleep. Though time and the six year difference in their ages had driven them a bit apart, Luke still remembered that night, still loved his sister for being there for him when he'd needed someone to comfort him.

"No," he said, shaking his head to clear the memory of that nightmare away. "No, I didn't."

She put her hand on his shoulder. "Well, that's how Phoebe is, you know that. She'll probably never change."

"I know," Luke sighed. "I just hoped that maybe this time would be different."

"One day, maybe, but that ain't today. And where's the cookies Alexis sent?"

"On the counter."

"Did they all make it here?" she asked, getting up and walking into the kitchen.

"*Yes*, they all made it here. Mostly."

"Uh huh." Rebekah sat back down next to him.

"So how are the kids?" he asked, tearing into the last piece of fish.

"Off with their dad this week, but they're good," she said between cookie bites. "Michelle got accepted at Prairie View, so that's where she'll be going next year."

"That's good, but with her grades," – Luke's niece had taken every award her high school had except for "highest GPA by a boy" –"why not go somewhere more prestigious?"

"They had the best chemical engineerin' program, so that's where she wanted to go."

"Hard to believe she's already a senior. I remember when she was born."

"That's 'cause you gettin' old."

"What about Albert?" Luke finished the last piece of fish and took the plate into the kitchen.

"That boy. Lord, I'll be lucky if he graduates high school at all."

"That bad, huh?"

"Yeah. I dunno what to do with him. He just can't seem to settle down and study, wants to run 'round with his thug-ass friends all the time."

Luke smiled. "Reminds me of you in school, you liked to go out all the time and party, too."

"That's 'cause I *had* friends, unlike you an' Matthew." There was a smile in the barb; Luke knew it was jokingly delivered and no sting intended.

"You also got beat on the ACT test by a seventh-grader, as I recall," he shot back, equally playful.

Rebekah laughed and softly punched his arm. "All right, smart-ass," she said. "You gonna wait 'round for Momma and Matthew to get back?"

"No. It's been a hard day; I think I need to get back to the hotel and detox from talking to Phoebe, maybe use the hotel gym. Plus, I haven't talked to Sierra today, so I need to call her."

"Yeah, I saw the grave was dug already."

"Werner did that. Speaking of which, I don't suppose you're coming to the wake or funeral or anything, are you?"

Rebekah looked down at the table. "Naw, I'm with Alexis on that. I just don't see the point. All that stuff was over and done a long time ago - for most of us." She stood up suddenly. Luke stood with her, guessing she meant to walk him to the door.

Luke tilted his head at her as they walked into the kitchen. "What do you mean?"

Rebekah opened the kitchen door for him. "I mean ... it's like him leavin' the rest of us alone gave us time to put him behind us, right? Well, except really for Phoebe and Matthew, and Momma, and Billie and Christopher.... Okay, it gave me and Alexis and Danette time to put him behind us and move on. You didn't get that time, since you were the one he kept in touch with and, really, you was the one he came back for. I know him not bein' here hurt everybody, but me and Alexis, we just, I dunno, we just got over him.

Matthew and Phoebe and all them, including you, never did."

Luke nodded. "That makes sense, I guess."

Rebekah gave him another hug and a kiss on the cheek. "Oh, that reminds me. I need Sierra's number. It's a book I'm looking for that she might have, and I can prob'ly get it cheaper from her."

"Oh, okay," Luke replied, pulling out his phone as Rebekah pulled hers out of a dress pocket. He rattled off the number quickly, and checked her phone to make sure she'd entered it correctly. "You goin' out tonight?"

"Yeah, I am. I get the kids back Sunday, so I'd better enjoy my time off from parentin' while I can, you heard?"

Luke laughed a little as he closed the door softly behind him. He thought back over the events of the day as he walked to the car; a progression from sister to sister, and realized it had taken both Alexis and Rebekah to truly make him feel better after the unfortunate confrontation with Phoebe. *Maybe it takes both of them to balance her out on a universal scale.*

But then, who balances me *out?* he wondered, as he exited the driveway and headed south, towards Riverton, towards the hotel room that was somehow more comfortable, more familiar, more welcoming than the house he'd grown up in.

CHAPTER FIVE

Not much of a view, Luke thought as he lit his first cigarette of the day.

In front of him, across the parking lot, an earthen levee rose 50 feet, its grass-covered side littered with scattered brown leaves. From the walkway in front of his hotel room, he could see the tops of the casinos on the other side, tethered to the levee and floating in a small lake that connected to the Mississippi River a few miles away. Though he could only hear a vague murmur of crowd noise, he knew that, since it was Saturday, the casinos would be crowded, filled with people hoping for their lucky break, the win that would turn their lives around. They kept chasing a dream that lived on, no matter how many times they went home with empty pockets and strained livers.

Some people in the community had been unhappy when the casinos came in, Luke remembered: the objectors decried a possible perversion of their city, something Luke found entertaining, given Riverton's drug, gang, prostitution, and alcoholism problems. What was really left to pervert in Riverton?

Watching a crowd below him, gathered around a sign that read "Casino Shuttle Pick-up here – Every 30 minutes," Luke had to wonder if there wasn't something to that – for people from neighboring states that didn't have casinos. The people of Riverton, though, had adjusted quickly to the new businesses and enjoyed the jobs and tourism money the casinos brought in. As for those in Riverton that were regular patrons, Luke suspected the cause of their frequent visits wasn't so much gambling addiction as it was sheer resoluteness, a fierce determination to try, over and over again, what they thought was their way out of here.

That was the one good thing about Riverton: the people were generally poor, ill-educated, and mired in lives full of trouble, but they never gave up hoping for more, trying for better. In a strange way, that was the point behind all the drugs and prostitution and gangs: people doing what they could with what they had to improve their lives, issues of legality aside. The attempts rarely succeeded, but people never gave up trying. Even the homeless people Luke had seen fighting in the dumpster the day before were trying to improve themselves or defend what they had acquired.

Even with that admirable resoluteness throughout the city, however, Luke still wanted to get the hell out of Riverton. The resolve was admirable; the wreckage of that resolve's failures was not. The streets of Riverton were made of hopes and dreams, but populated with the shambling, endlessly resolute ruins of those dreams. Most people fell in the gap between the two, but that gap had a fierce downward slant. Luke reflected on how easy it was to fall down and how hard it was to get back up as he put out his cigarette and lit another.

The wake didn't start until 6 PM; it was only 12:30 PM, according to his watch. He wanted to go out to Constance's house before the wake, to try once again to get her to go with him. Luke was a believer in closure, and felt that being part of this process would help everybody close the door on James Jackson forever. He doubted anyone would go, but he had to try anyway: resoluteness was just in his blood – or was it just hard-headed persistence?

Luke felt an acute ache for his grandmother suddenly. She would have gone to at least the funeral with him, if not also the wake. She'd had no affection at all for James – *I still need to ask Constance about Grandma threatening to shoot him* – but she would have gone to support Luke. She would have helped with the costs of the funeral as well. She had always been a giving woman. That habit had no doubt helped her keep the far-spread extended Washington family together in spirit, if not physically.

But she was gone, and no replacement had popped up. Constance just wasn't as forceful, and her talent lay in other, far less visible directions. None of Luke's aunts had stepped up either. Now that he thought about it, he supposed his uncles could have filled her shoes, but she was such a quietly imposing matriarch to the family that it just seemed natural her replacement, if she had one, also be female. And so, the family had drifted apart after her death. Luke had only been back to Riverton once since her death four years ago, and that had been a quick visit while attending the funeral of Sierra's uncle in Arkansas.

It's not the same without Grandma. Riverton just did not feel like home without her – not that it had felt a lot like home with her, either. Luke watched a short white bus pull into the parking lot; below him, the crowd at the sign erupted in cheers. As they filed onto the bus, Luke stubbed out his cigarette and returned to his room.

As he tossed his bathrobe onto the bed, Luke wondered what his grandmother would have done. She would probably have tried again to get people to come to the wake, but then again, she wouldn't have had to try hard the first time. People just didn't say no to her. Not for the first time, he wished he'd had the same gift. She would never have had to beg for people to help pay for the funeral; she would not have had to ask anybody to attend. Luke felt a pang in his heart. He missed her very much, and regretted not learning more from her while he'd had the chance.

He picked out black jeans and a white t-shirt to wear for now; he'd put on his dress shirt and tie later. As he pulled the t-shirt down, his stomach growled. "But first, she'd get something to eat," he said aloud.

****

"So what's going on in the morning?" Luke asked Sierra as he drove down Framer's Point Road. The time was 5 PM in Riverton, meaning it would be 3 in Seattle. Before heading out to the farm, he'd spent some time driving around Riverton, checking out his old haunts. Not many of them were left: the roller-skating rink had been boarded up, the bookstore had closed down, the corner market had been demolished to make room for a sign announcing the hospital's presence. The only thing really left was the mall, and almost a quarter of the storefronts in it had been empty.

"I need to get up and be at the shop early tomorrow." Sierra replied on the other end of the phone line. "Expecting

someone to come in about some of the first editions, and it's
an early appointment. I'm gonna try gettin' to bed early, so I
might not answer if you call after the wake." There was a
little waver in her voice as she spoke. Luke was unsure of its
import, but he'd have to figure it out later; he was at the
house and turning into the driveway.

"Eh, okay. If we don't talk later, goodnight, honey,
sleep well and sweet dreams. I love you."

"Thanks. I hope the wake goes okay. Love you too," she
said, and hung up. Luke got out of the car, now parked in
Constance's parking spot; her car was again missing. Luke
half-wondered if she'd had a change of heart and left for the
wake without him, but certainly she would have called and
told him so, if only to spare him from driving out here? But
no, when he knocked on the door, she answered and opened
the door. She wore blue jeans and a faded Riverton High t-
shirt, not the sort of clothes one would wear to a wake – at
least not in the South, where appearance was damn near
everything.

"Where's your car?" Luke asked as he stepped inside.
He had finally made his own attire presentable by putting
on a white dress shirt and black tie over his own white t-
shirt, though he kept the black jeans on, preferring to save
his suit for the funeral.

"Matthew took it to town. He had some dry-cleanin' to
pick up and said he wanted to get some art supplies. "As she
talked, Constance walked from the kitchen into the living
room and took her place in Luke's grandmother's chair.
Some sort of talk show was on the TV; Luke briefly glanced
at it and dismissed it before sitting down on the couch.

An uncomfortable silence hung between them. Constance appeared to be watching the talk show intently. Luke fiddled with his wedding ring, smoothed out his jeans and shirt, straightened his tie, checked his watch, fiddled with his ring again.

"Well?" Constance asked, breaking the silence.

"Why aren't you going to the wake?"

Constance sighed deeply, a sound Luke hated. It made him instantly regret asking the question. Wherever Constance might have fallen short in comparison to Luke's grandmother, she easily outpaced her mother in the Guilt-Inducing Sigh category. Whereas Luke's grandmother had a more wistful sort of regret-inducing sigh, Constance's sighs sounded to Luke's ears like Sisyphus and Atlas singing a particularly mournful Negro spiritual. It was as if the cause of the sigh, usually him, was to her the weight of the world, a boulder that refused to stay uphill, and a vicious slavemaster all rolled into one. "Naw," she finally said. "Naw, I ain't goin'."

"Why not?" *It's already paid for.*

"Luke, he wasn't a good man. I know he was your father, but he just wasn't a good man. You grew up to be so much better than him. I wish you hadn't wasted yo' money on takin' care of him."

"We're past that now —"

"No, *you're* past it." Constance's voice held an unfamiliar edge to it. "But that was always you, always movin' faster and thinkin' faster than everybody else, and movin' past things faster, too. You didn't get scarred by him like the rest of us did. Give the rest of us time to … do what we need to, too."

Luke barely kept himself from rolling his eyes. She blamed James alone for Luke's scarring, as if James was the only parent that had damaged him. "There's only going to be one wake and one funeral, Mother. It's a chance to get closure and move on. To say goodbye to all the pain. I'm all for people healing and grieving in their own time, but this chance only comes along once." She'd already had years to get over him, and had many more in front of her – why wouldn't she want this chance for real, physical closure?

Constance pulled her glasses off with one hand and pinched the bridge of her nose with the other. "You think seeing him dead, layin' there all lifeless and waxy-lookin' in a coffin, is gonna make everything better all of a sudden?"

"You have to admit," Luke said with a shrug, "it's something you haven't tried yet."

Constance burst into laughter. Luke grinned as she laughed, hoping behind his teeth that the joke had been enough to convince her to go. "You always were quick-witted, just like your Uncle Ned," she said, wiping tears of laughter from her eyes. Her voice, however, took on a dark tone. "I can't go, Luke. I just can't. Don't ask me again, please."

"All right," Luke answered, and slumped back against the couch, feeling defeated. There was nothing else he could do or say. He knew that, though he still felt his grandmother would have done better. "Where's Rebekah?"

"It's Saturday night, Luke, that girl could be anywhere. You wanna try callin' her?"

"No, I guess not. I'd better get going," Luke said, standing up. "What about the funeral tomorrow?"

"I don' know yet. We'll see. Check back in the mornin', and then we'll see. I ain't promisin' nothin', though."

"All right," Luke said, bending to give his sitting mother a hug and a kiss on the cheek. "Oh hey, I wanted to ask you — did Grandma threaten to shoot James a few years ago? Is that why he moved in with Billie?"

All traces of Constance's smile left her face. Her eyes turned dark before leaving Luke's face to intently study her hands, which lay folded in her lap. "Yeah. She did."

Luke's brows furrowed. "Why?" He asked the question even though he was afraid of the answer. Had there been another incident like the one he witnessed when he was younger?

****

He'd been no older than six when it happened, not long after the death of Letitia but before her brothers had made it clear that their threats against James were not empty words. He'd been at home that night with Grandma, James, and Constance; he couldn't recall where Rebekah and Matthew had been when it happened. He'd been in the living room, watching TV with Grandma, when they'd heard James and Constance arguing in the back bedroom, the raised voices creeping swiftly into shouts.

Grandma had sent him to see what was going on. He'd walked down the hallway as carefully as he could, trying not to make any noise, trying not to draw their attention – or anger – to himself. He crept up to the doorframe and peeked into the room just in time to see James shove Constance against the dresser, then saw Constance rebound quickly to shove James back … and that was all he'd seen before he ran down the hall, away from the frightening, violent adults and back to the comfort of his serene grandmother. When he told her what he'd seen, she told him to go back and tell them to stop. He didn't want to, was afraid to, but somehow the notion that he was acting for his grandmother made it easier, made him braver.

When he returned to the bedroom, they were still shouting and shoving, and he delivered his message in as strong a voice as he could muster. They'd ignored him, continued shouting and punctuating their words with shoves as though he hadn't spoken at all. He returned to his grandmother and told her of this as well, feeling himself a failure because he hadn't stopped them. Grandma, on the other hand, hadn't seemed to feel much of anything; she hadn't even stopped reading the newspaper while the fight had been going on. "Tell them *I* said to stop," she'd said, rattling the paper as she turned it to another page, not even looking at Luke.

He'd run back to the bedroom, emboldened again by the sense of mission from her, slid into the bedroom on the attached footies of his Batman pajamas, and had spoken, clearly but softly, "Grandma said to tell you *she* said to stop."

They'd stopped immediately, frozen in place: arms raised, mouths open, staring at him like he'd suddenly sprouted wings and antennae—but obeying like he'd borne a message from God.

****

"Was there … was there another fight?" Luke asked softly. He'd often wondered if there had ever been more, but had never worked up the courage to ask. Maybe, he wondered of himself in his darker moods, he simply didn't *care* enough to ask.

"No," Constance said, "nothin' really like that." She picked up a digital clock from the table. "It's 5:40. You better get goin'."

Luke shrugged in defeat, and got up from the couch. "I'll check back in the morning."

In the garage, he petted Bingo, who was warming up to him. Bingo repaid the gesture by walking Luke to his car. All the way to the funeral home, Luke wondered what happened, why his grandmother might have tried to shoot James. He ran every possibility he could through his mind and came up with nothing plausible. It was unlikely that James had gotten into a physical altercation with an old woman. Grandma had never been fond of James, but she wasn't the type to lose her temper without strong provocation. What could have pushed her over the edge into actually trying to shoot James?

The questions raced through his mind as he parked the car in the Kirkman lot and got out. *No more time for questions,* he thought, looking at the front of the building. *Time to go see the man with all of the answers.*

Luke doubted, however, that James would be sharing those or any other answers today. Or ever again.

****

". . . so we'll be closing it up about 9, is that cool?"

"Yeah, that's fine. I don't think a lot of people will be here. It's not like you're gonna be turning crowds away. Any other viewings going on tonight?"

"Nope," Tim said. "It's October, it's kinda our slow season." Tim's eyes were rimmed with red; from tears or alcohol, Luke could not say, and did not want to ask.

"How does a funeral home have a slow season? Or a busy season, for that matter?"

"It happens, my nigga, it happens. I'm gonna go do some paperwork" — by which Luke figured he meant 'go drink in the privacy of the office' — "and check on you later. The guestbook is just outside the door, and this is the only open viewin' room, so people shouldn't have trouble findin' it. You cool?"

Luke looked around the room. It seemed like a fairly large room, about 30 feet from the entrance at the rear, where Luke and Tim were standing, to the other end. James lay in his casket at the other end, the top half open, a leafy green wreath with "Rest in Peace" written in gold on a white banner across it. The soft lighting reflected nicely off of the wood-paneled walls, and the cream-colored carpet looked comfortably soft. The table that held James' casket had been decorated with a floor-length white skirt with gold trim, presumably to match the wreath, and presented a nice visual contrast to the dark wood of the casket itself. Five rows of pews, with red velvet padded seats and a burgundy-carpeted aisle in the middle, looked like they could comfortably seat about sixty people. All in all, Luke thought it was pretty impressive, especially for the discounted price. It struck Luke as quite a shame that nobody else would see it. "Who sent the wreath?"

"Oh that," Tim said with a sly smile. "We keep a few 'round for cases like these. Not everybody can afford flowers for funerals and shit, especially not in this poor-ass town."

"Oh. Well, it's nice. Thanks for that, Tim. And for the big room. We're not gonna need it, though."

"Hey, nothin' but the best for my family. That's the perk of workin' here." Tim patted Luke's shoulder as he turned to leave. "I already said my goodbyes, I'll leave you two alone for yours. Lemme know, you need anything." He left Luke alone in the viewing room. Alone with James.

Luke sighed. Now that they were alone, there wasn't any point to putting it off. He strode up the aisle slowly, fingers brushing the ends of the pews on either side as he walked. Luke studied everything as he went: the carpet in the aisle, the carpet under the pews, the maroon curtains behind his father's casket, the exposed rafters that gave the room a rural but dignified atmosphere, anything and everything but the casket until he was finally directly in front of it, and could ignore it no longer.

He looked down. James laid there, his caramel skin looking just a little waxy, the warm, deep dark brown eyes he'd shared with some of his children closed forever. He still had a full head of hair, though most of it had gone grey. His mouth was closed, covering the toothy grin he used to flash, and his lips appeared to be curved in a slight smile. No more laughter would come from that mouth, not even the chuckle he'd passed on to Luke. The suit Billie had given Luke for the funeral looked immaculate; Luke guessed it had been dry-cleaned for the occasion. The older man almost looked alive, almost like he was going to jump up and announce this was all a big joke.

Luke waited.

James did not jump up and announce that it was a joke.

"Well, James," Luke said, "how are you going to get out of *this* one?"

James did not answer.

Luke looked around the room. No one had teleported in.

"I guess you're not getting out of this one, huh?"

James still did not answer.

"I mean, this is it, the Big Chill, the finale, the great mystery. You're really gone."

James lay still in his casket.

"You're gone, and we never got to talk, never got to work shit out. I always meant to … always meant to call or something, maybe stop by Billie's on a visit … and now it's too late. Wait, you know what? Fuck that, *you* could have called *me* too. It's not just my fault. You could have reached out, too."

James didn't speak, move, fidget, anything. Luke sat down in the nearest pew, elbows on his knees, his palms together in front of him, fingers entwined.

"You didn't call, you didn't write, nothing. I know it wasn't just Sierra. We'd had that talk about my white friends before, that was why we hadn't talked much before I married her. What else was it? Why else did you stay away from the child you said you'd 'try your best to do right by'? I don't think you did right by *any* of us, given the fucking mess you left behind you. Phoebe and Matthew won't speak to me. Danette moved away and wouldn't even come back for this. Alexis and Rebekah made peace with you and still aren't here. Christopher's looking for a Heavenly Father to fill the hole his real one left. Billie and Constance both hate you. No, James, I don't think you did right by *anybody* you left behind. But here I am, five thousand dollars poorer, because I couldn't be you. Because I had to do right by somebody who didn't do right by me."

Luke dabbed at his eyes, looking up at the unmoving form of James. With his head outlined by the white satin of the casket's lining, he looked almost angelic. Maybe that was why caskets always had white linings? He'd have to ask Tim later.

"You know, Billie and Constance, both of them think I shouldn't have done anything. They think I should have left you for the county to take care of. Phoebe too. None of them understood that I *had* to do this.

"But Grandma would have understood. Even though she apparently threatened to shoot you, I don't know why, she would have understood me making this trip to take care of you. Even though I'm not sure *I* entirely understand why I did it, she would have understood. She would have said 'you do what you can for family' and that would have been the end of it for her, but I don't know that that's why I'm here."

Luke sighed. "Maybe Phoebe was right. Maybe it *was* guilt for turning away from you. Maybe it was me, just wanting to do for family. Maybe it was just a need for closure, to talk to you face-to-face before you – your body, at least – went away forever. More likely, it was all of the above – plus Paul pushing me to come."

James still didn't respond, leaving Luke's words alone to hang in the air.

"Fuck's sake, James," Luke said, his voice weary, "why'd you have to be such a shitheel?

"I mean, I guess it wasn't really the racism that bothered me so much. It's Mississippi; there are a lot of racist people here. It was just that," Luke sighed deeply. "*You weren't there.* When I was growing up, and getting picked on in school by the black kids for such dumb reasons: I look mixed, I didn't speak like them, I was smart, I have freckles, I was quiet, I read comic books, I didn't live in the neighborhood, any neighborhood really, all just a bunch of stupid bully reasoning that all came down to one thing: *he is different, he must be punished.* That's really what all bullying comes down to anyway, isn't it? Punishing the different. You weren't around for any of that; you left town because Letitia's brothers wanted your ass – well, they wanted you then where you are now. And I can understand needing to leave, not wanting to stick around and get killed.

"But you weren't there for that. You weren't there to defend me or tell me how to deal with bullies of any color. And for you to come back – when I'm in college, no less – and try to tell me not to be so close with white people, that they'd turn on me? When they were the people in school that *didn't* bully me, that were nice to me and hung out with me instead of mocking and bullying me? Maybe they were only friendly to my face, I don't know. But that was better than the black kids being bullying assholes to my face.

"In the world you grew up in, you had reason to believe that, sure, and be distrustful of the white kids, even when the black kids were being dicks to you. But that wasn't *my* world. And I sure as shit wasn't going to have you trying to tell me that twelve years of school were wrong, that I had to hang out with the black kids because the white kids weren't to be trusted, when it was the black kids who beat me up and pushed me around and made school suck for me. I wasn't going to have you tell me that my experiences were wrong. They weren't. You would have known that — *if you'd been there.*

"But you weren't. You weren't there when *I* truly needed you. No amount of money makes up for that, no amount of money fixes that. Yet I'm here for you, when everybody else abandoned you. I'm here, 2,500 miles away from a woman I love dearly and you could never accept, I'm here having paid five thousand dollars just to see your dead ass buried instead of burned, for a man who tried to be a father when I'd already raised myself … and maybe I'm here …"

Luke stood up, walked to the casket, and leaned in close to his dead father's face.

"Maybe it is guilt. Maybe it is closure. Maybe it is Paul Cussler pushing me. Maybe I'm here because you failed all of your children as a father and all your known lovers as a partner. But really, some little mean part of me thinks that, maybe, just maybe, I came here to tell you one thing.

"I'm better than you. I'm a better man, a better spouse, and hopefully one day, I'll be a better father. Most parents raise their children to have better lives than them, maybe even be better parents. Maybe that was what you wanted. Well, that was the end result, not because you raised me, but because books and comic books and bullies and my grandmother raised me, and they all made me what I am today: *better than you.*

"I hope you can hear me, wherever you are. I hope you take that knowledge through whatever eternal torment or endless void you're traveling through now: your son is better than you, and it's *in spite* of you, not *because* of you."

James did not reply, but to Luke's wet eyes, he seemed to be smiling a little less, the curve of his lips seemingly straighter, into more of a hard line.

****

"Are you dead?"

Luke started at the question. He had returned to the first pew after talking to James and merely sat there silently, waiting for someone to come in. No one had.

Until now, apparently. Luke shook his head to clear the cobwebs.

"No, ummmm, no, 'm not dead-" he replied, then looked up, and realized the question had not been directed at him. Someone stood in front of the casket, their back to him.

"Are you dead, you withered shit?" Luke opened his mouth to call out to the new arrival, but before he could say anything, a loud smack reverberated through the viewing room. The new arrival shouted "Wake up!" and slapped James again. "Wake up, you fucker! You don't get to die!"

Luke started to stand, then recognized the black pinstripe suit that hung loosely off its wearer, the unkempt afro, and the slightly pointed ears so much like his own. The man was not as big as he used to be, a difference that threw Luke off for a second.

"Matthew?" Luke asked, shocked into stillness, still half-risen in the pew.

Matthew ignored him. "Wake up! You don't get to fuck up my life and then *die*!" Another slap. Luke saw Matthew's arms reach into the casket and close around James' neck. "You hear me? You *ruined* my fucking life!"

Luke could hear feet running outside; Tim must have heard the yelling. "Matthew!" Luke shouted, breaking out of his paralysis and stepping forward. Before he reached his brother, though, Matthew turned around, his face twisted in a snarl and saliva on his lips. The sight stopped Luke again, and made him remember the last time he had seen that look.

****

"Luke! They fightin', Luke, they fightin'!

That had been his play-cousin Rafael, yelling as they'd just been about to get into the car. It was near midnight on Christmas Eve, ten years ago, and Rafael, who lived a mile away, had come over to hang out. Grandma had gone to bed earlier, right after Gethsemane's Christmas Eve service. Matthew, home from college for the holidays, had been drawing at the dinner table, off in his own little world as always. Luke had been home from his freshman year at college. James, who had returned to live with their mother after Luke's graduation, had been looking at Matthew's art, offering comments here and there, which Matthew seemed to only acknowledge with grunts. That had been the situation when Luke and Rafael had stepped into the garage.

Now Rafael, who had glanced through the kitchen door window, said they were fighting? Who? Over what? "Lemme check this out, that can't be right," Luke replied. He stepped back into the kitchen, Rafael close behind him, and what he saw shocked him into immobility.

Rafael had not been mistaken.

"Fight" was too mild a term for it. Matthew and James were locked in mortal combat by the kitchen sink. James was losing badly, losing more than the fight. His arms flailed ineffectually at Matthew, who had his hands wrapped tight around their father's neck, as he screamed incoherently, spit flying as he ranted and choked the life out of James. Matthew had been bigger then, which Luke had thought was mostly fat, but apparently there was more than enough muscle behind it to overpower James and enough adrenaline in Matthew's blood to completely ignore James's already-weakening attempts to knock him away.

There was no mistaking what was happening here. Matthew was not merely fighting James. Matthew was *killing* James.

Luke broke from his shock first, and rushed towards the fighters. "Go get my mother!" he barked to Rafael, who ran out of the kitchen every bit as swiftly as Luke ran in. He aimed a punch at Matthew's head as he ran, a quick jab to the temple to stun him, make him let go.

Matthew turned his head just in time to catch Luke's arm in his teeth.

What the fuck, Luke thought, staring at his arm, trapped between his brother's teeth. He could feel each tooth pressing into his forearm, holding it fast. None had broken the skin, but they would, with just a little more pressure. And the pressure on James' throat hadn't relented at all. Luke could see the muscles in Matthew's neck straining, thick and quivering with his brother's rage. He tried to reach around and pull Matthew's arm away with his left hand instead, but couldn't do it. Matthew was too broad, Luke's arms too short.

"Matthew!" a voice screamed. Luke tore his gaze away from Matthew. Constance stood in the doorway, next to Rafael. She was screaming at Matthew to stop, to quit it, to let them both go, but he didn't listen. He was in the grip of a terrifying rage, strangling his father and biting his brother and her words would not interfere with that. Luke was still trying and failing to pull Matthew away or pull his arms down, the teeth in his arm were beginning to hurt. James's struggles had grown weaker still, and the only person in the house that Matthew actually talked to had no power over him.

But Luke knew of a higher power in the house — or at least a more heavily-armed one.

"Get Grandma! Bring her gun!"

Later, Luke would agonize over those words for years to come, and he thought probably he would for the rest of his life. What had he really intended? Just to scare Matthew into stopping? Or had he really hoped, in that moment, for his grandmother to shoot his brother? He knew his grandmother; she had several guns and, Luke was pretty sure, wouldn't hesitate to use one to save a life, even James's. Or maybe Luke only intended her to show the gun to scare Matthew? He asked himself that question over and over again, trying to recall what he'd been thinking in that split second, and never came up with a conclusive answer. The only thing he knew for certain was that he'd said the words, and whatever his intent had been when he said them,

"Get Grandma! Bring her shotgun!"

"No!" Constance yelled, stopping Rafael in his tracks. Luke's shout had stirred her to motion, and that wasn't the only thing it had done. As she crossed the brown kitchen tiles, Matthew's rage left him. He released James and Luke and collapsed, sobbing, into his mother's arms.

"Shame on you, Luke, calling for her to bring her gun!" Constance said, her arms around Matthew. Rafael and Luke were supporting James, who was breathing in deep, hitching gulps, trying to get his legs back under him.

Shame on me? Luke lifted his father to his feet. *I'm not the one who attempted patricide.* But he didn't say what he thought. He rarely did to Constance, even then. He stood there, supporting his father and watching his mother comfort Matthew, for only a few seconds before his brain kicked back into gear and figured out a plan.

"Get his other arm," Luke told Rafael, "we're staying at your house tonight." Without another word, they helped James out to Constance's car and eased him into the backseat. As he got into the driver's seat, Luke heard Rebekah's voice, heavy with sleep, ask Constance what had happened. Luke wondered what answer she'd gotten as he backed the car out of the garage and into the darkness of early Christmas morning.

At Rafael's house, Luke had explained the situation to Dennis, Rafael's father, who agreed to let them spend the night. As soon as James could talk, though he did so with a bit of a rasp, he asked to use the phone. Dennis agreed to that as well, and offered him some coffee to calm his nerves. Luke didn't ask who he called or listen to the conversation; instead, he'd gone into Rafael's bedroom, pulled out a sleeping bag, and crawled into it, hoping not for sleep but to wake up from this nightmare.

In the morning, he and James went back to Constance's house just long enough to brush their teeth and for James to get his things, and then Luke, who had neither hide nor hair of a driver's license, took James to Phoebe's house, where he lived until after the following summer, until Matthew returned to college.

****

"Luke! Fuckin' *help me*, nigga!"

Tim's shout pulled Luke from his memories. Luke blinked to wipe them away and saw Tim in front of him, his scrawny arms wrapped around Matthew's left arm, trying to pull him away from the casket. Matthew's right hand was still in the casket, still on James' throat, trying to block air that James no longer needed. Though Matthew was no longer as big as he'd been, the rage made him just as formidable. Scrawny as he was, Tim was clearly not going to be able to pull Matthew away by himself.

Luke wrapped his arms around Matthew's right arm. "Pull back!" he commanded Tim, and they both did, pulling

Matthew away from the casket – but he didn't relinquish his grip so easily. As they moved backwards, so did the casket, caught in Matthew's grip as Luke pulled the hand away from James' neck. It slid from the table and crashed to the floor, wood bursting in chunks from the corner as it smacked against the carpeted concrete. With the rest of the casket leaning against the table still, gravity worked its magic; James slid forward out of the coffin, his head coming to rest on the carpet as Tim and Luke half-carried Matthew out of the viewing room.

"Let me go!" Matthew bellowed as they dragged him to the door and tossed him out of the funeral home, into the parking lot. He didn't gain his footing in time, and fell to the asphalt.

"What the fuck is wrong with you?" Tim said. "You come back in here, I'm calling the fucking cops, nigga, bet on *that* shit."

"*Shut the fuck up!*" Matthew hissed, struggling to his knees. Luke saw water on Matthew's face and wondered if he'd been crying, then noticed that the whole parking lot was wet. Looking up at a streetlight, he saw a gentle rain falling. "You don't know what he did to me!"

"I do," Luke said quietly. Both Matthew and Tim turned to look at him. "He's dead now, and he can't hurt you anymore."

Matthew glared at Luke as he got to his feet, but said nothing else.

"He's dead, Matthew. Let it go, for your own sake, please."

Matthew said nothing, only glared at Luke and Tim as he got into Constance's car.

Luke and Tim watched him go in silence, watched the taillights of Constance's car as it roared down the street. "What the fuck was that all about?" Tim asked as he straightened his shirt and tie. "That nigga was *pissed*. If looks could kill-"

"If looks could kill, you'd hire him to go around glaring at people to help drum up business." Luke smiled weakly at his own joke.

"Yeah, maybe, if he wouldn't come shit all over the services." Tim held the door open for Luke as they walked back inside. "For real, though, what was that all about?"

Luke shrugged. "It was ... just a man trying to kill his demons."

"Did he have to do it here?"

"Wasn't my choice to make," Luke replied, straightening his clothes. "Come on, I'll help you get things set back up."

"Don' worry 'bout it," Tim said. "There's a director on his way in with a pickup, I'll have him help me. You care about the damage to the casket?"

"Nope. Not like anybody's going to see it anyway."

"Cool." Tim checked his watch. "Look, it's after 9, the viewin's officially over. You can go, I gotta close up and clean up."

Luke looked back towards the viewing room. "Yeah, I think I'm gonna go. It's been a rough day."

"All right, be here at 11, we'll head down for the funeral."

"I'll meet you at the church. No point in a hearse-and-one-car funeral procession, is there?"

"I guess not, then. See you at Gethsemane." Tim stuck his hand out. Luke shook it warmly.

"See you there," Luke said, then stepped outside. Tim locked the door behind him, the sound of the bolt sliding home ringing with a ridiculous finality in his ears.

As he climbed into the rental car, Luke thought about calling Sierra, just to have someone to talk to, then remembered that she'd gone to bed early. Though he hated the idea of waking her up, he couldn't think of anyone else to talk to about what had happened. Everybody that knew his father wouldn't care, and those few that knew Matthew wouldn't want to hear about it.

"Hello?" Even sleepy, Sierra's voice still held its beautiful Southern accent.

"Hey," Luke replied, pulling out of the parking lot. "Sorry to wake you up, but I just – I didn't have anybody else to call."

"It's okay," she said. Luke could picture her clearly, rubbing sleep away from her eyes. "What's going on?"

"I just left the wake."

"How did it go? Did you get to say goodbye?"

Luke stopped at a red light. "I did, yeah. So did Matthew."

"Matthew showed up?"

"Yeah, Matthew showed up, and tried to choke the shit out of James."

"*What?*"

"It won't make any more sense the second time," Luke answered, turning onto Washington Boulevard, a street clearly named by someone with delusions of grandeur. "He tried to choke our dead father."

"Jesus, Luke, why?"

Luke sighed as he pulled into the hotel parking lot. "I don't think – I don't think Matthew likes himself very much, and I think he blamed James for being the way that he is."

"What way?"

"What could make being a black man in the South even more difficult?"

"Chasing white women?" Luke could hear her smile.

"Not chasing women at all."

"Oh?" she replied, then it sank in. "*Oh.*"

"Yeah."

"How long have you known-"

"Since college, when I found his porn collection." Luke set the rental car's alarm and set off towards his room.

"And you never thought to tell me?"

"Wasn't my secret to tell."

"Fair enough, but – we are going to have to talk about how much you hold inside, Luke. I'm your *wife*, you should be able to trust me. Not only that, but you carry too much inside. We should be sharing all our burdens, Luke – not that I'm not guilty of keeping things inside, too, but we both need to work on that."

Luke knew his wife was right. Neither of them talked much about their pasts, mutually preferring to enjoy the present of their lives together, and that needed to change. "You're right, Sierra, I'm sorry. I just don't want to dwell on the past, but it feels like I've time-traveled back to it."

"Just talking and sharing isn't dwelling, Luke, it's opening up. We'll talk about it later. How are you?"

"Hang on," Luke said, and took off his shirt. "Okay, I'm back. I don't know how I feel. I don't know if that helped Matthew or not. I don't know – I feel bad."

"Why?"

"Because I'm not that angry at James, and I feel like I should be."

"Why?"

He sat down on the bed to take off his shoes and pants. "Because everybody else is."

"Maybe you moved past it?"

"I don't think I ever was that angry at James. Never mind how angry Matthew was; I'm not even at Christopher-levels of angry."

"Maybe you just dealt with it better?"

Luke sighed. "I don't think I dealt with anything very well at all. Look at how fucked up all my family relationships are: Matthew Phoebe, Constance, even Christopher, who at least actually likes me. They're all fucked up and I can't fix them."

He could hear Sierra's frown of concern through the phone. "You're being too hard on yourself. I *know* you, Luke, I know you've tried the best you can to fix things. But you're just one person, baby, you're just one man. You can't fix everything."

"Thanks," Luke replied. He smiled a little at her encouraging words.

"You're always telling me to be kind to myself; well, do the same for you. You're not perfect, you've made mistakes, but you're one man. I'm sure you did your best. You always do. But you can't fix everyone, or everything." There was a sound of sheets rustling as Sierra moved in the bed. "Honey, I'm tired. . ."

"Me too," Luke replied, stretching out on the bed. "It's okay, love. I'll call you tomorrow. Sleep well and sweet dreams, dear heart."

"Love you."

"Love you too."

When Sierra hung up, Luke was left alone with his memories and thoughts, his least-favorite company. He stared at the ceiling, waiting for sleep to overtake him.

He stared for a long time, Sierra's words rolling around in his head.

Pandem Buckner

CHAPTER SIX

Luke woke up Sunday morning with a fierce desire not to be in Riverton.

He closed his eyes tight, tapped his heels together and murmured, "There's no place like somewhere else." He opened his eyes again, and found himself still staring at the ceiling of his hotel room.

"Goddammit," he said. He swung his legs out of the bed and stood up. One more day, and he could go back to Seattle, back to Sierra, back to his life.

As he showered, the memory of the wake hit him full force and he groaned. He hoped Matthew had gained some sort of catharsis from the post-mortem strangulation, but he doubted it. At least Tim would have an interesting story to tell for years to come.

After getting dressed in a black suit, white shirt, and purple tie, he was ready to go. Still, he felt unprepared for the day, and looked around the room trying to figure out what else he could do. There was nothing left to be done.

"How does one prepare for a father's funeral, anyway?" he asked no one as he walked to the car. No one answered.

****

Luke pulled into the driveway of Constance's house as he hung up his phone. He'd tried calling Sierra, but she hadn't answered. He'd tried calling Rebekah as well, to get an idea of the state of things at Grandma's house, but she also didn't answer. He figured she was probably sleeping off her Saturday night.

He stared at the kitchen door through the open garage. Bingo stared back at him, his canine head tilted quizzically. He didn't *want* to get out of the car, didn't want to have to deal with Constance's questions about last night or Matthew's probably-surly attitude. Constance's car was there, so he was reasonably certain both of them were home. Rebekah's car was gone, which didn't surprise him at all.

Luke kept staring at the door. Bingo tired of their staring game and went back to licking himself. The shovel stood where he'd left it, right next to the kitchen door. No one had come to the door or peeked through a window when Luke pulled up. He wondered if they even knew he was there. His eyes still on the door, he picked up his phone and called Constance.

"Hello?" she answered.

"Hey, it's me," Luke replied. "I'm, um, running short on time, so I thought I'd call and ask if you'd changed your mind about going to the funeral." He doubted she would have, but he wouldn't feel he'd really done everything if he didn't give her one last chance.

124

"What happened last night? Matthew came home upset and won't come out of his room!"

Fuck. "He didn't tell you?"

"No, he didn't." She paused. "He said to ask you."

"He came to the wake and tried to kill James all over again. It took both Tim and I to drag him out of there."

"Oh Lord," Constance said, and Luke could hear her expression: eyebrows low, eyes downcast, lips curved into a frown. It was a very "woe is me" expression, and it annoyed him every time he saw it. "You shouldn't have got involved, Luke, look at all the mess you stirred up."

"*I* stirred! I ... grrrrr," Luke said, biting his tongue. "Look, are you going to the funeral or not?"

"Naw, I ain't goin'. It'd just stir up more—"

Luke cut her off. "Okay then, I'm gonna stop by and grab the shovel. I'll talk to you afterwards, I'm sure." He hung up before she could respond, and slammed the car door as he got out. *How was last night my fault? All I did was try to give the guy a decent send-off, how am I the villain here? Because I remembered somebody that everybody either wants to forget or wants to kill again?*

He snatched the shovel from its resting spot, startling Bingo, who took his bone in his teeth and slunk away to the other side of the garage. *Bloody fucking hell, I'm just trying to do the right thing, and it feels like I'm being blamed for everything he did. But that's not exactly new, is it?* Luke climbed into the driver's seat and slammed the door closed behind him. He clenched and unclenched his left hand, trying to relieve some of his stress through the motion, and breathed deeply several times. The last deep breath hitched on its way out, and the small shudder helped Luke collect himself. "One more day," he told himself. "One more day. I can do this."

His composure regained, he started the car and drove off, more eager to attend a funeral than talk to his mother again that day.

****

When Luke arrived at the church a few minutes later, he saw that Tim had already arrived. The hearse was backed up to the concrete porch of the small white cinderblock building, its rear door propped open. Tim and a funeral director stood at the front of the hearse, smoking cigarettes as they waited for him. By the time he opened the car door, the men were trying ineffectually to wave away the dust clouds his car had kicked up from the gravel road.

"Damn, nigga, you tryin' to smoke us out?" Tim asked, coughing and flapping his hands.

"Just road dust. You get used to it." Luke stood next to the men and lit his own cigarette as he gazed at the church.

Gethsemane Baptist Church had always looked to Luke like an old-time schoolhouse: squat, rectangular, and bordered by one gravel road, a small cemetery in the back, and cotton fields all around. It had a small steeple over the front door, just a white wooden cross that added maybe three feet to the height of the building, and an extension of the maroon-tiled angled roof jutted about four feet past the front door, covering the concrete patio.

Luke remembered coming here every second and fourth Sunday for worship with his mother, grandmother, and siblings, at least until they (and he) were old enough to occasionally opt out of church by being somewhere else on Sunday morning. The bars covering the air conditioners were new to his eyes, though he remembered his mother telling him years before that they'd had problems with people stealing them. *A church literally as poor as its mice, and yet people still stole what they could from it.* He shook his head at the thought of someone wanting to rob this tiny little church.

Also new to his eyes was the fellowship hall his uncles had built two years ago, giving the building an L-shape where it jutted to the north from the rear of the building. Two pecan trees, one at the north edge of the grass-covered clearing and the other at the western edge, on the far side of the building from Luke, supplied the brown leaves that dotted the grass.

"So what do we do?" Luke asked. "We just wheel him in, or what?"

"It's four of us here: me, you, Joseph, and Reverend Kane is inside. We can just carry him," Tim replied, stubbing out his cigarette on the bottom of his shoe. He yelled into the church, his voice projecting easily through the open doors, "Yo, Reverend Kane! Come help us carry this muthafucka!"

Reverend Kane emerged from the Pastor's Study, just inside the front doors. He was taller than Luke by a good six inches, with very short hair, very dark skin, dark bloodshot brown eyes, a wide mouth and a wiry frame. He wore a black robe, with a white shirt collar and the knot of his tie poking out from the top of the robe. Luke thought he could smell Old Spice as the Reverend approached. "This must be Luke," the gaunt preacher said, extending one bony, gnarled hand towards Luke. "Reverend July couldn't make it, so he asked me to fill in. I'm very sorry about your loss, Luke."

Luke gently shook the preacher's hand, feeling every single bone, muscle, and vein in the man's hand as he did. It was a very unsettling feeling, almost as unsettling as having those slightly-bulging, dark, red-rimmed eyes focused upon him. "Umm, thanks, Reverend, for agreeing to be here."

"You know, I go where the Lord sends me, Luke, as do we all." He released Luke's hand and turned to Tim. "And you need to watch your mouth, son, we're on God's land."

"Ain't all land God's land?" Tim retorted. "'Cause if it is, I can't say shit anywhere on Earth."

Luke turned away, so that the preacher wouldn't see him laughing, and saw a truck driving down Framer's Point Road, towards Constance's house. While he was too far away to make out the exact model of the truck, the clouded noon sun was bright enough for him to make out its grey-green colour. It looked like Werner's truck, but Luke couldn't imagine why Werner would be going to the house.

"C'mon, Luke," Tim called. "You get the right side, I'll get the left." Tim stood at the back of the hearse, his hands on the casket, sliding it forward enough for them to get a good grip on it. "I'll take the damaged corner."

Luke considered the scrawniness of the preacher. "Tim, are you sure we shouldn't get the back?" The funeral director, a silent caramel-skinned man with a low afro, was big, rotund in fact, but Luke was not sure how much of that muscle was mass and how much was just fat.

"Naw," said Tim, getting his shoulder under the casket. "We his family; *we* lead the way."

With Tim and Luke at the head of the party, the four men carried James' casket into the church. Luke couldn't help looking around as they entered, with doors on the left leading to the pastor's study and secretary's room, and both doors on the right leading to the small kitchen. Luke and Tim both reached forward to open the swinging double doors that led to the main hall of the church.

The main hall was more twice the size of the viewing room at the funeral home. A frayed red carpet muffled their steps as they walked past the rows of orange-painted pews with bibles and songbooks on racks in the back of each one, past the eight orange-tinted windows evenly spaced along the white cinderblock walls, until they finally arrived at the front of the church. The table from the viewing, complete with its gold-trimmed white skirt, had been placed directly in front of the pulpit, which stood on a raised, carpeted platform, with chairs behind it for the pastor and deacons or guest pastors. Behind the chairs were two rows of seating for the choir.

They placed the casket atop the table gently, Luke and Tim setting their corners down gingerly in concert with Reverend Kane and Joseph, the funeral director.

"Should we open the casket?" Tim asked Luke.

Before Luke could answer, Joseph spoke, in a deep bass voice that rumbled from his barrel chest. "I think, yeah, we should have it open."

"Why?" asked Tim. "Nobody's here but us."

"I did a really great job on him, I'm kinda proud of it."

Luke shrugged. "Go ahead." As Tim opened the casket and locked it in the open position, Luke took a seat in the front pew. *The wreath looks nice here, too* . He was glad Tim had remembered to bring it. Though the church was still empty save for himself, Joseph, Tim, and Reverend Kane, the wreath did make the place seem a bit more like a proper funeral than a rote ritual for a man no one loved.

Reverend Kane took his place behind the podium. "Let us bow our heads in prayer," he said; Luke and the others immediately obeyed, Luke more from habit than genuine devotion.

"Lord, we gather here today to send one of your children home, Lord, James Jackson, who you sent to this earth" — Luke heard papers shuffling at the pulpit — "62 years ago, Lord, and in that time he was a carpenter, a truck driver, a husband, and a father. Now, Lord, we send him back to you, asking you to have mercy on his soul, Lord, and on the souls of those people that James" — more papers shuffled — "Jackson has left behind on this cold, cruel world. Lord, we ask Your Holy kindness and grace on him and ourselves, Lord. These and other blessings we ask in the names of the Father, The Son, and The Holy Ghost, rest, rule, and abide henceforth and forevermore, let us all say together: amen."

"Kept it brief," Luke whispered to Tim, who sat close to him on the front pew.

"You ain't payin' him by the word," Tim replied.

"My sermon today," Reverend Kane began, "comes from the book of Corinthians...." Luke tuned out, looking at his father. Would he appreciate this, or would he too think that Luke had wasted his time and money? It certainly was everyone else's opinion. Maybe not Matthew's, though he hadn't even thanked Luke for giving him the chance to strangle their father again. *Maybe he'll send me a card or something.* And Billie and Christopher — he could relate to Christopher's struggle, definitely. But for Billie to blame Luke for Letitia's demise when she — and Constance — were the women who had aided in her humiliation ... maybe blaming him was easier than accepting their own responsibility? Maybe it was the same for Matthew, that it was easier to blame James for the struggles he endured than accept himself as he was? But then, what about Phoebe? Was it just the death of her mother that she hated James for? Or did she, too, blame him for her own actions, for becoming a promiscuous alcoholic?

And what was it about Rebekah and Alexis that allowed them to be so at peace with their father? It wasn't religion; Rebekah didn't seem to care about any religion one way or another. It wasn't partying and having fun with friends; Alexis didn't drink or go out on the town much. Was it that they had children of their own? No, Christopher did too, and he had been largely unsuccessful in his search for peace. So what did they have inside them that Luke did not?

And how could he get it?

"Luke," Tim said, tapping Luke on the shoulder. "Luke, you're on."

"What?" Luke asked, startled out of his thoughts.

"Luke, you're on. You gotta give the eulogy."

"Eulogy?" Luke hadn't even thought about the eulogy. "For what? There's nobody here! Besides, you knew him better than me, you do it." Luke also hated making speeches, but this didn't feel to him like a good time to mention that. He looked up and saw Reverend Kane looking at him, his gnarled hand extended.

"Luke, me and James was family, we was cool, but you were his *favorite*." That word rankled deep in Luke's heart. "I know if he had the choice, he'd ask you to do it." Luke knew Tim was right, and didn't like it.

"We hadn't talked in *years*, Tim—"

"We ask again that the son of the deceased please come up and say a few words to help celebrate his life," Reverend Kane intoned in his raspy, creepy voice. *Might as well ask me to come to the dark side.* The thought forced Luke to suppress a wholly inappropriate smile.

"I ... I can't ..."

Tim clasped Luke's shoulder firmly. "You *can*, you *should*, and Luke, I think you *need* to."

"What could I even say? I was just as mad at him as – well, not Phoebe or Matthew – but he was just as big a bastard to me as anybody."

"Y'all need to quit trippin'," Tim replied, a deeper sincerity in his bloodshot eyes than Luke had ever seen there before. "Y'all made him more than he ever was. He was only ever jus' a man, just like you, just like me. Talk about that."

Luke stared silently at Tim. Was he right? The idea boggled Luke's mind. All the things his father had been to him and others in his life – could James Jackson have been merely a man, at the bottom of it all?

"Luke?" Reverend Kane asked.

"All right," Luke replied, turning away from Tim. "I'll give the eulogy."

****

Luke hated public speaking, even in front of such a small crowd. He hoped the anxiety didn't show as he stepped up onto the dais. Reverend Kane said nothing while Luke approached; he merely retreated from the pulpit and settled into one of the high-backed chairs in front of the choir seating, off to Luke's left. Luke took his place behind the pulpit and stared out into the church.

Tim sat in the first row of pews, on the right, where Luke had been sitting. Joseph had seated himself in a pew against the wall to Luke's right, a place usually reserved for the ushers. Luke looked to his left and saw the two empty pews that were reserved for special guests and the church's Council of Mothers, a collection of elderly women that oversaw church business. In the closest of the two pews, Luke could see three small white pillows with black crosses stitched onto them, each one representing a deceased member of the Mother Council. The third pillow was the only one made from satin instead of cotton, and bore ornate stitching.

That pillow, Luke had placed there himself. He'd asked a friend in Seattle to make it for him, and she had, stitched it well and made it to last. It had flown with him from Seattle to Little Rock, ridden in the rental car with he and Sierra, waited a few days in the hotel room while they visited family and friends. Finally, Luke had brought the pillow here, his tears falling onto it as he'd placed it in his grandmother's seat.

He felt tears welling in his eyes, a wave of grief at his grandmother's absence. Her wake had packed the funeral home; her funeral was a standing-room-only affair, and even then, nearly as many people stood outside of the church as stood inside. She had been the matriarch of both the church and of her family, larger-than-life yet down to earth, short in stature but powerful in personality. Many missed her, many mourned her.

But today, there were no mourners. Only those obligated through conscience or cash had gathered for James Jackson, patriarch of nothing. The contrast left a hitch in his chest.

Luke tore his eyes away from the pillow and looked forward. He opened his mouth to speak, found it dry, closed it. He held his eyes closed for a long moment, then opened them again. He could still see Tim in the front pew, and Joseph in his periphery, but that was all. He opened his mouth again, but nothing came out. He looked again towards the pillow, wishing his grandmother was there. *She* would have known what to say; she would have known how to be honest and kind and fair, even to someone she didn't like. Luke didn't know how to do that, and this was not the time to learn.

Tim moved, drawing Luke's attention. Tim placed his right hand on his chest, fingers splayed, and reached forward and slightly upwards with his left, his head leaning back and mouth wide open, a pantomime of a dramatic actor on the stage. Luke chuckled, and the chuckle that rolled from his lips sounded like his father's voice.

That chuckle took him back, to the days of barbecues and fun trips to the movie with James, to the few, dear good times they'd had, before everything went to shit, before James had become the villain of so many lives. What could anyone say about a man who'd been so many things to so many people? What could be said that would be honest but fair?

And Luke knew what to say.

"'Friends, Romans, countrymen, lend me your ears," Luke said, intending to continue but finding himself unable to speak, surprised into silence by a familiar creak from the other end of the room.

The doors to the main hall swung inward.

CHAPTER SEVEN

Three women entered the church, and the first—from that distance, the way she carried herself, her height, her smile when she saw him ...

Grandma?

Luke blinked, unable to believe his eyes. When he looked again, the woman wasn't his grandmother. For just a moment though, while he'd wanted to be fooled, while he'd wanted his grandmother there so badly, she'd looked so much like a younger version of his grandmother.

But she wasn't.

It was Rebekah, in a black dress, just knee-length, that looked similar to those the church's ushers and Council of Mothers used to wear, with a black hat that he was pretty sure had been pilfered from their grandmother's closet; the pink carnation on its right side and the loose netting around the brim looked very familiar to him. Somehow the combination of dress and hat and skin tone made her look a little younger than her years, though the glasses and dress called attention to the strong resemblance to their grandmother.

Behind her, on her right, walked Alexis, taller than Rebekah and also wearing a knee-length black dress. She looked tired. Her eyes seemed darker than normal and heavy, the skin around them wrinkled and dark. Luke didn't think she had looked so tired Friday, but he couldn't be sure.

And the third woman, behind Rebekah, to her left...

Her black dress matched the dresses of the other two, but clung to her curves a bit better, due perhaps to her smaller frame. Her sensuously-wide hips, smaller waist, and generous bosom were well-defined by her dress, her waves of dark brown hair capped with a black pillbox hat that he had never seen before, and that was when he knew her. The black provided an interesting contrast to her pale skin, making her look younger than she was, though Luke knew she was the youngest of the three. Of them, she alone seemed well-rested and unworn, though a slight lessening in her smile and a wariness around her eyes told him that she was not entirely comfortable with the circumstances. Despite that, she still took his breath away; she always did.

Sierra, here in Riverton, here in his family's church. Her going to bed early the night before made sense now; she must have planned this with Rebekah. Luke had and hadn't wanted to her to come, but now, seeing her, he was glad of her presence.

The three women walked down the well-worn carpet and took seats in the second row of pews, to Luke's left. He smiled at them, trying to figure out how and when they'd arranged this. He tried to speak, stopped, tried again, stopped.

Rebekah made a rolling motion with her fingers. *Right*, Luke thought. *Get on with it.*

"'Friends, Romans, countrymen, lend me your ears,'" he began again. "'I come to bury Caesar, not to praise him.'" Tim raised an eyebrow at that, but Luke continued. "'The evil that men do lives after them; the good is oft interred with their bones …' but for James Jackson, let it not be so."

Quizzical now, Tim tilted his head. Alexis and Rebekah slowly nodded. Sierra gave him a tired smile, and Joseph, as near as Luke could tell, was asleep.

"James wasn't perfect by any means. He wasn't a good father to his children, he wasn't a good husband to either of his wives, he wasn't always attentive to family and friends. We know all that. I've seen for myself this week, in talking to my own siblings about his death and this funeral, just how much the ill – I can't call him 'evil'- has lived on after him. I've seen the loathing, anger, resentment, and even outright hatred that James managed to produce in others in his lifetime. Even his death seemed to have done nothing to reduce, never mind eliminate, those feelings in people."

Tim nodded at that.

"But it feels like no one remembers the good that James did at all. He helped create his children. He stayed married to his first wife for 15 years; surely there had been some good in that time, enough to keep her there? And yes, that time was marred with his own infidelity, which I understand she never knew about until shortly before her unfortunate demise, but in that time, surely there were smiles and laughter and playtimes with her daughters that kept her fears and suspicions allayed?"

This time, it was Alexis who nodded, her tired eyes tinged with sadness and memory.

"And I know there were times when he did things and had fun with his other children as well. Those incidents aren't common, but to me, that rarity makes them all the more valuable, all the more worth focusing on in remembering James the man.

"There *must* have been good in him, for anyone to ever have trusted and loved him, even if only for a short time, for so many people to pin their hopes and hearts and dreams onto just one man. I can remember how — some people would light up, knowing he was coming to visit during his trucking days, as though he was bringing the solution to all their problems with him. When he left, and those problems were still there, that was okay, they would get better next time. What mattered most was that little problem-free island of his visits, and no amount of disillusionment would shake the hope that somehow, he would make things better, at least for a while."

Rebekah put a hand over her face. Luke knew she remembered those days as well as he did.

"But he wasn't the answer to all of anyone's problems. He was not some reborn Messiah, coming to save the day and make everything better. James Jackson was no angel, no Savior, no hero. He was just a man.

"And later in his life, after the tragic death of Letitia, after he was forced to flee for his very life, he became vilified. It was as though the good he did in life was largely interred with the remains of Letitia. To some, he became an evil figure, someone who destroyed worlds, who took life and hope and love away to leave bitterness and lies and delusions in his wake, the cruelest of villains who only knew how to hurt, never to help. He became a nightmare, a boogeyman, a devil without peer."

A tear crept down Alexis' face. Phoebe's severe demonization of their father had been hurtful to more than just herself, Luke knew. But, to some extent, they'd all demonized James, even if they'd later forgiven him.

"But he was not the cause of all of anyone's problems. He was not Satan born on Earth, come to ruin lives and break hearts. He was no devil, no Leviathan, no villain. James Jackson was just a man."

The words rang true in Luke's head, in his heart, in his soul. He looked at the dead man in the casket in front of him and kept speaking.

"That's all he was. That's all he ever was, ever could have been. Just a man. He made a lot of mistakes, but he made a lot of people happy in his lifetime, too. That happiness might have been temporary, but so what? *All* happiness is temporary, just as all misery is temporary. He didn't live up to all of the expectations and hopes many people projected onto his shoulders, but who in this world has ever been capable of doing that? Who has ever been perfectly good or perfectly bad? Who has never caused inadvertent harm to another or never once done something to help others? Who in history has not ever disappointed others?"

Luke paused to wipe his eyes. Behind him, he heard Reverend Kane say, "That's all right, keep on." In front of him, Tim and the three women nodded agreement. Luke cleared his throat and continued.

"I didn't know James Jackson as well as I should have. Until I had to take care of this, I didn't even know when his birthday was. I hadn't talked to him for years before he died, and that is both our faults. But I wonder sometimes if maybe he wasn't showing his love and respect for me by keeping a distance, by letting me grow and become my own man, in my own way, a way more suited to the world *I* grew up in rather than indoctrinating me into the world and ways *he* grew up in. I'd like to think he knew he could never change who he was, and maybe, just maybe, to give his children better than he had, he stayed out of their way. And in that, at least, he largely succeeded. None of his children are like him, and I think *that*, most of all, was what he wanted."

"It's not for me to say if the price he paid for that was worth it. I didn't have to pay it, so it's not fair of me to judge it."

"None shall judge but Him above," Reverend Kane said. Luke nodded at him in acknowledgement, and continued."

"But we - his children, his lovers, his family, all those he left behind - are as we are, and for that, we should not blame nor credit James Jackson. For that, we bear sole responsibility. We had no choice in what we perceived as being done to us, but how we react to what happened, to what was done, how we let it affect us, in those things we have *all* the choice, all the decision, all the power. And how have we used that? Some used it to become better people, some to wallow in misery, some to never move on from the moments of pain. Some, I fear, will never move on past James and grow. And that's - well, it's not all right, but it is what it is. We too are just human."

"Amen to that," Tim said. Everyone else either nodded or said "amen" as well.

"Like James, like every human, we have to do the best we can with what we have. I believe that with all my heart, that the most that can be said of anyone is that they did the best they could with what they had, and in a fair number of cases, it is *all* that can be said of someone. James never had much. He didn't have much money, education, or worldly knowledge. He didn't have much self-discipline or true betterment opportunities. But he did as well as he could with what he had."

Luke felt his eyes dampening again. He looked at Sierra and saw her hands over her heart, a gesture she used to mean that she felt and understood what he felt. Her eyes were wet as well.

"He made us laugh. He made us feel good. He made us forget our problems, even if just for a little while – hell, even if he *caused* the problems, he could make you forget them for a little while. That was his gift, that was what he had, and he did the best he could with it.

"I quoted before that I had come not to praise Caesar, but bury him. That's not entirely true. I am not burying Caesar today; I am only trying to bury the *illusion* of Caesar. James Jackson was not an all-powerful being, inflicting good and ill on people from on high." Luke knew that none of the people present felt that way about James, but that wasn't the point. All Luke wanted to do was speak the truth about his father, for James, for himself, for all the wasted years.

"He was not God, he was not Zeus, he was not Satan. James Jackson was just a father, a husband, a carpenter, a truck driver. And eventually he was an old man who died unloved and unwanted for the crime of not being more than he was.

"But, first and foremost, James Jackson was just a man. And that is who I bury today."

His vision blurry, Luke stepped swiftly and silently away from the podium, amid applause from the others gathered there. Tim tried to get his attention as he sped by, but Luke did not stop. Instead, he walked down the aisle to the second row of pews, where Sierra stood waiting for him, her arms open. He hugged her fiercely, tightly, greedily.

Only when her arms closed around his shoulders, when he felt the love and heat and warmth of her against him, did he allow the sobs held in his chest to break free.

****

After making sure the casket was securely strapped down and locked into place, Tim closed the rear door of the hearse, then stepped over to Luke while Joseph slid behind the driver's seat.

"They don't let you drive?" Luke joked, his voice still slightly wavering.

"Naw," Tim replied. "You wreck one durin' a funeral and that's pretty much the end of that." He put his hand on

Luke's shoulder and gave it a firm squeeze. "That was a great eulogy, man, you did good for him."

Luke felt the tears about to flow again, but he reflexively swallowed them. He stood with one arm around Sierra's waist, keeping her close as they stood on the church's small porch. Rebekah and Alexis had run off to the restroom once the service ended, denying Luke the chance to ask them any questions. Reverend Kane had gone off to his own car, parked on the other side of the hearse, and waited patiently for the hearse to lead the way to the cemetery. "Thanks, Tim. So what now, we just follow you to the cemetery?"

"Yeah. You know, we got to get the rack and everything set up, so why don't you maybe take a few minutes 'fore you head over? Collect yourself and shit." He spoke to Luke, but Luke noticed that his eyes were on Sierra; Luke understood what Tim meant.

"I think I will. I could use a little break."

"Alright, then—hey, there's my girls!" Tim said. Luke turned to see Rebekah and Alexis walk around the corner of the church, the sisters looking almost cheerful despite the redness of their eyes. Luke watched Tim run over to them and gave them both big hugs.

"Are you okay?" Sierra asked, in a low voice.

"I am now," Luke replied, giving her a kiss on the cheek. "So how exactly did you end up here?"

"Oh, well, it's a bit of a story. Rebekah called me Friday and said you might need some help here, that things were kind of rough, and asked if I might be able to make it down here for the funeral. It was a little sudden, but I was able to get a red-eye for last night. Rebekah picked me up in Little Rock—"

"I wondered where she was last night."

"Yeah, she and Alexis were picking me up this morning. Then we had to eat breakfast, and went shopping for a dress for Rebekah, and I needed a nap badly, we all did, so that's why we were late. We all overslept a little. Sorry for being late."

"It's okay," he said, kissing her cheek again. "You showed up at just the right time."

Rebekah and Alexis came over to them. Luke let Sierra go to give Rebekah a tight hug. "Thank you, sister, for arranging this." It was, Luke felt, what their grandmother would have done.

"Ain't no thang," Rebekah replied, smiling.

"It was somethin' to *me*," Alexis said. "I couldn't sleep much, drivin' with her to Little Rock, keepin' her up when she was drivin', havin' to walk through that damn airport. I bet I look like hell."

"Not so bad," Luke said, hugging her and kissing her cheek. "Alexis, I'm really glad you decided to come. You and Rebekah." He gave Rebekah a kiss on the cheek as well. Behind them, the hearse pulled out of the churchyard and onto the gravel road. Reverend Kane's small car was swallowed by dust clouds as he followed the hearse. Luke did his best to wave the clouds away from his sisters and wife. "Why did you two come? I thought you weren't going to."

"Well, that was partly me," Alexis said. "I thought about it, and thought about it. It actually kept me up some; I couldn't sleep for thinkin' about it. I finally thought it wasn't right for nobody to be there for him, whatever he did, or *didn't* do, as you pointed out to Phoebe. Plus, I hadn't met Sierra yet."

"It wasn't all *you*," Rebekah snorted, playfully smacking Alexis' arm, making her jump. "I thought about it too, after I called Sierra. In the end, I decided that, you know, we have to do for family." Luke couldn't help smiling; those words were what had brought him back to Riverton.

"So you came for me?" Luke asked.

"Naw, don't get no big head. I brought Sierra for *you*, I came to the funeral for *him*."

"Good enough," Luke replied, and hugged his sister again.

"We better get on to the cemetery, girl," Alexis said to Rebekah. "It's startin' to rain out here." As she said it, Luke noticed the few drops falling around them, increasing in frequency as he watched.

"So? You just *look* like chocolate, you ain't *made* of it," Rebekah retorted, though she started moving towards her car. "I got an umbrella in here, come on."

"I'm coming," Alexis replied. "We'll see y'all at the cemetery."

As they watched his sisters drive off, Luke turned to Sierra. "So now you've met Alexis."

"She seems pretty nice. Once we figured out to stay away from talking about religion, we got along good." Luke opened the passenger door of his rental car for her. "Why didn't she come to the wedding?"

Luke waited until he was in the driver's seat to answer. "Things were a little tense with that side of the family then." He started the car and backed out onto the gravel road. "More my fault than hers. I think I was just angry at all James' children."

"Huh. Oh, who's Phoebe?"

"Alexis and Rebekah didn't tell you?"

"I kinda slept a lot on the way here."

Luke sighed. "Phoebe is a long, nasty story in an albino cover with dyed blond hair."

****

By the time Luke and Sierra arrived at the cemetery, everybody else was ready. The casket was in place above the grave, held there by an elaborate contraption of metal bars and straps that Luke knew would lower it gently into the grave. Alexis and Rebekah stood next to Tim at the side of the grave, all of them hiding from the shower under Rebekah's umbrella. Reverend Kane stood at the head of the open casket, his Bible in his hands, an umbrella nestled in the crook of his arm. Joseph had wandered off to the northern end of the cemetery, opposite the mourners; Luke wondered why until he saw the phone in the round man's hands. As they were walking away from the car, Luke suddenly remembered the shovel and had to go back to get it.

Once they had each taken a place, Reverend Kane began his speech. "Oh Heavenly Father, we commend unto you the spirit and body of James Jackson ..." James looked peaceful, Luke had to admit. He didn't know whose idea it had been to re-open the casket, but he was glad they had done it. He hadn't been able to look at James much during the funeral, and he would never get another chance after this. Though this slightly-waxy stillness was not the way he would remember James, it still felt important to him to remember this moment, remember this passing.

"'Never forget the face of your father,'" Sierra whispered beside him. The reference made Luke smile.

"... let us all say together, amen."

"Amen," the mourners said. Luke watched Joseph return, putting his phone away, and whisper briefly to Tim, who came over to Luke.

"Hey, you done good," Tim said, putting a hand on Luke's shoulder. "You did him proud."

"Yeah," Luke said. He watched as Joseph lowered the lid of the casket.

"Wait," Sierra said.

All eyes turned to her.

"I ... we didn't have time to stop for flowers, so I made one," she said, pulling a carefully folded piece of paper out of her purse. "I just, I thought it would be something nice to give him," she said, blushing. Luke knew she hated being the center of attention.

Luke smiled and kissed her cheek. "Go ahead," he said, and walked beside her to the casket. Gingerly, she placed the paper flower on the satin pillow besides James' head.

As they stepped away from the casket, Luke said, "That was really nice of you – I should have brought something too."

"That's all right," Rebekah said as she approached the casket. "You've done more than enough, Luke. And I didn't bring anything either." Instead of placing something in the casket, Rebekah bent low and gave James a kiss on the cheek. "Goodbye, James," she said softly, so low Luke could barely hear her. "Goodbye, and I forgive you."

Tim came next. His eyes redder and wetter than normal, he reached inside his jacket and pulled out a flask. Luke fully expected him to pour some out in honour of James; instead, he surprised Luke by placing the flask inside James' jacket pocket. "Peace out, my nigga," Tim said with a cracking voice. "I'll see you when I get there."

Alexis came last, a pair of scissors in one hand and several dark strands of something in the other. "Bye, Daddy," she said, and placed the strands on the pillow; once she let them go, Luke could tell that they were strands of her hair. "May the Lord have mercy on your soul. I love you. I forgive you."

Luke blinked back tears as he hugged his sisters again. He still felt bad about having nothing to put into the casket, but Alexis assured him that it was okay. While they hugged and talked, Joseph closed the casket lid, locked it in place, then began turning the crank that lowered the casket into the grave. Alexis and Rebekah wept as James was lowered below the grave's edge; Sierra held Luke's hand tightly between hers as they watched. When the casket was all the way down, Joseph disengaged some mechanism, then rolled up the straps and quickly disassembled the machine.

"Hey, we gotta go. Joe's gotta make a pickup." Tim said, wiping his eyes. He gave Luke a stronger hug than Luke thought the scrawny man could ever have managed. "You leavin' tomorrow?"

"Yeah, I – we – got a long trip back, so I'm looking to leave early."

"All right then, my nigga," he said, shaking Luke's hand. "Don't be a fuckin' stranger, you heard?"

Luke couldn't help smiling. "I heard," he replied, "you too." Reverend Kane was next, wagging a stern finger at Tim as he shook Luke's hand.

"I'm going with them," Kane said in his raspy voice. "I know the family they're visiting; they'll be in need of comfort—and I fear young Tim is *always* in need of spiritual guidance."

"Good luck with that, Reverend," Luke said, shaking the older man's hand. Though it was still as gnarled as before, it didn't seem quite so creepy now. "And thank you for everything."

"It was God's will I was here; I'm glad to have had the chance to serve it well." With that, the Reverend went off to his little car and drove off, the engine sputtering as it trailed behind the hearse.

"All right," Luke said, taking off his jacket. "Sierra, can you hold this?"

"What are you doing?"

"I have to fill the grave in. That's why I had him buried here, to save on having to pay gravediggers."

"Oh," Sierra replied. "Well, can't we help?" She looked down at her clothes. "On second thought, if you give us a few minutes, we can go change and come back to help?"

"I got it, honey," Luke said, feeling suddenly sad for some reason as he rolled up his sleeves. "Besides, I only brought the one shovel."

"We could, I don't know, take turns ..." Her voice trailed off as Rebekah put her hand on Sierra's shoulder.

"Let him do this, Sierra," Rebekah said, her eyes still full of tears. "I think this is why he's really here."

"Besides, it ain't like I ain't done it before," Luke said, remembering his grandmother's funeral. "Except it was raining harder then."

As the three women huddled and chatted under the umbrella, Luke got to work with the shovel, lifting out loads of dirt from the mound beside the open grave and depositing them on top of James' casket. He was careful to spread the dirt around, moving from place to place to make sure the hole was filled evenly. *Shuuuf.* Another load of dirt filled the shovel. *Thumpf.* The load fell atop the casket.

Shuuuf. Another load picked up. *Thumpf.* Another load dropped.

Shuuuf.

Luke remembered one birthday, when James got him a bike as a present. Luke had really wanted a Knight Rider talking car, and been unable to conceal his disappointment.

Thumpf.

But Luke had ridden and kept the bike for seven years, long after his interest in Knight Rider had waned.

Shuuuf.

Other memories came to mind as Luke lifted and dumped, lifted and dumped.

Thumpf.

They'd had a barbecue, was it on Memorial Day or the Fourth or Labor Day? Luke couldn't remember, only that he was 4, almost 5, and saw his mother, in matching green and blue-trimmed shorts and shirt stealing a kiss from James, and they both seemed so happy.

Thumpf.

Rebekah, 11 or 12, coming home from school one day, excited about her new friend Alexis.

Shuuuf.

Months later, Rebekah and Constance crying after a phone call from Alexis, Werner taking Luke outside with him. "Uncle Werner, what's going on? What's wrong?"

"Somebody died, Luke, somebody ... fell off the bridge."

Shuuuf.

Young Luke, 8 years old, asking Constance where James was, why he hadn't seen him in a long time.

Thumpf.

The first phone call from the road, from James' exile: "I sent you a hundred dollars by Western Union."

Shuuuf.

Luke on the ground at a park in Riverton, hurt and confused, his lip bleeding, his eye aching; some boys pulling a screaming, crying Phoebe off of him as his mother ran over, trailed by Phoebe's uncle.

Thumpf.

"Why do you have to leave again?"

"Some people are looking for me, son."

"Why?"

"You wouldn't understand."

Shuuuf.

Getting ready for high school graduation.

"You made it!"

"I did, son, I did, but I didn't bring you a present. Here, you can borrow my camera and take pictures, though."

Luke never returned the camera.

Thumpf.

"Luke! They fightin', Luke, they fightin'!"

Shuuuf.

Phoebe scowling at him as he drove away after dropping off James.

Thumpf.

Luke and Christopher and James all together in St. Louis, at the Jackson family's first and only reunion. That had been a happy week, the first he'd spent around his brother and father simultaneously. They'd also brought Luke's college girlfriend Isabelle, and Christopher teased him for years afterwards about the sound of the headboard hitting the wall between their rooms and keeping him awake. But James never said a word about it.

Shuuuf.

Years later, at a Cracker Barrel in Arkadelphia, Arkansas, where Luke went to college: "I'm just saying, they'll be good friends, but when push comes to shove, they won't stand by you. . ."

Thumpf.

Luke walking out of the restaurant, to his (white) friend's house across the street, staying there until he was sure James had gone back home.

Shuuuf.

At Billie's house, a couple of years later.

"I'm engaged. This is Sierra," Luke said, handing over a picture of them together.

James frowned. "Aw man, why you gotta go and marry a white woman?"

Thumpf.

All over now, it was all over now, all of that, all of James Jackson's life, over and done with, finished ...

Shuuuf.

All of it now the past. All of *James* was now the past. All he had ever been, ever could have been, was buried now by time, memory, and this last shovelful of earth.

Thumpf.

It resounded with a certain unmistakable, undeniable finality, that last mound of dirt. *Like Death's final due, like change placed in a dead man's mouth for Charon, like the final shot of a long war, like the Bell of the All-Over. . .*

It is all over.

James *is all over.*

"And my work here is done," Luke said aloud.

The three women, who had been talking and sharing pictures on their phones while Luke had been shoveling, looked at him, then at the filled-in grave. Sierra spoke first: "Did you bring extra clothes? You're soaked!"

Luke looked down at himself, realizing that she was right: his clothes were soaked clean through, clinging to him tightly. He hadn't noticed as he'd been filling the grave; in fact, he'd completely forgotten that it had been raining at all. "Ugh," he said, holding his arms out. "Yeah, I did. We'll go up to the house and change."

"Give me the keys," Sierra said, holding her hand out as Luke took them out of the pocket of his slacks. "I'll drive so you don't get the seat driver's seat all icky. Maybe you should sit in the backseat — what's so funny?" she asked Alexis and Rebekah, who were smiling and trying to hide their amusement behind their hands.

"Nothing," Rebekah replied, smirking. "It's just, we've never heard anybody tell Luke what to do without gettin' a smart-assed comment back."

"No kiddin'," Alexis added. "Next thing you know, he'll be saying 'yes, dear' and wearin' pants all the time like a *civilized* person."

"I save the smart-assery for my sisters," Luke said, unrolling his sleeves. "And I *do* wear pants all the time. It's cold in Seattle."

They all laughed, and walked off towards their cars.

As he clambered into the backseat, Luke looked back at the cemetery. Despite the laughing people that had just left, it felt very lonely again. A gentle breeze whispered around the tombstones and the falling rain was muted as it landed on the fallen leaves. The solitary pecan tree maintained its vigil, undeterred by the recent activity, bare branches waving in the wind. "It almost seems a cruel place to leave someone," he said, holding the door open.

"Where?" Sierra asked as she started the car.

"Here. Out of sight, all alone, abandoned by the wayside as we move on with our lives. They just get left here, gone from the world."

"But never forgotten, Luke," she replied.

"No," he agreed, closing the door. "The good or the evil, it's never forgotten." *And how many will remember the good in James Jackson, and hold tight to it? How many will dwell on the ill and hold tight to it, letting it eat them alive? How many will find peace in his death and make peace in their lives? What will truly live on after him?*

"Whatcha thinkin', sweetie?"

"'Here was a Caesar!'" Luke said as they drove away. "'When comes such another?'"

CHAPTER EIGHT

After changing into a t-shirt and black jeans, Luke nestled into the couch in Constance's living room, Sierra on his right and Alexis on his left. Rebekah had taken his grandmother's chair for herself. To Luke, she looked like she belonged there, in ways Constance never had.

"Where is Constance?" Alexis asked.

"I don' know," Rebekah said, taking a drink of water. "She didn't say she was goin' anywhere today."

"Wasn't that her car outside when we pulled up?" Sierra said.

"Yeah, it was," Luke answered, "but I saw Werner heading this way just before the funeral. Maybe he took her somewhere?"

"It's daytime, though. She can drive fine in daylight," Rebekah replied. "She wouldn't need Werner to go to town."

"Is Matthew here?" Alexis asked. "Maybe he'll know."

Both Rebekah and Luke turned to stare at Alexis. "That's a bad idea," they said simultaneously, making Sierra laugh.

"Why, what happened now?" Alexis asked.

Luke sighed and reached out for Sierra's hand. Feeling her palm pressed against his made it easier for him to talk about the wake. "Remember the corner of James' casket, where the wood was splintered and broken?"

"Yeah, I meant to ask about that—I figured you got the coffin cheaper for it."

"It was fine when I bought it. *That* damage happened when Matthew came to the wake."

"What? What did he do at the wake?"

"Well—" Luke began, but was interrupted by the sound of a key in the kitchen door. "That must be her."

"Hey here!"

"Hey, Uncle Werner," Rebekah called from her seat.

"Hey, Werner," Alexis said.

"Hey y'all," Werner called from the kitchen. "Is, uhhh, is Luke in there?"

"Yeah," Luke called back, getting to his feet.

"Luke! Can I get some help here?"

As Luke stepped around Sierra's legs, Werner came into view in the dining room. Unusually for him, he wore dark green slacks with a black polo shirt, a big change from his normal jeans and button-down shirt, and smelled faintly of cologne. Luke couldn't remember Werner wearing any kind of scent unless it was a really special occasion. More surprising than his attire and pleasant scent, though, was what – rather, who – he bore under his left arm.

Constance slumped against Werner, her arm slung around his shoulders, using him for support as the two of them limped into view. Her black dress looked almost a match for Rebekah's, save that it was more rumpled and sported some stains on the front that Luke was pretty sure had been her breakfast. Werner stopped at the entrance to the living room, apparently unable to make it any further with his burden. When he stopped, Constance woozily raised her head and studied the four people staring at her.

"Hey, y'all," she slurred. "Hey, 'Lexis, ain't seen you in a—Sierra, is that you? Oh hell, it is. I'm sorry, y'all, I wasn't expectin' company. I'm sorry ..."

Luke broke the stunned silence in the living room. "The *fuck?* Are you *drunk?*"

"HEY!" Constance yelled back. "Donchu talk like that to - yo' momma ..." She staggered forward, pushing herself away from Werner, her finger wagging in the general direction of Luke's face, and made it three steps before falling forwards.

Luke caught her by the shoulders before her face hit the tiled floor. Rebekah got up to help, but before she could, Constance threw up on the dull red tiles. Luke stepped back as far as he could while still keeping Constance from falling, until Werner reached down and got her legs. Working together, the two of them managed to lever Constance back to her feet and put her arm around Luke's shoulder.

"I'm sorry, y'all, I'm so sorry," Constance said, her head slumped against Luke's shoulder.

"Werner, how in the fuck did *this* happen?" Luke asked, his eyes turned towards the older man.

Werner raised his hands. "She asked me to take her to the VFW today. It wasn't till I saw y'all at the church I realized that she wanted to be gone during the funeral."

"Tol' you 'bout that mouth," Constance muttered, smacking her free hand feebly against Luke's chest.

"Stop that," Luke told her. "She doesn't drink, Werner, how could you let her get this drunk?"

Werner shrugged. "She a grown woman, ain't my place to tell her what to do. She did what she wanted. You got her from here? I gotta clean out my truck."

"Yeah, we got her," Luke replied, shuffling towards the hallway, supporting Constance as best he could. "Rebekah, would you help me get her into bed? Alexis, Sierra, would you two please clean up in here and help Werner with his truck?"

"I'll take care of in here," Sierra replied, rising from the couch. Alexis headed outside with Werner as Rebekah ran ahead of Luke to find something for their mother to wear to bed.

"Well, at least today can't get much worse from here," Luke said, mostly to himself, as he and Constance shambled down the long hallway to the back bedroom.

"Thass right," Constance slurred.

****

"Matthew? Is that you?"

Luke grimaced at Constance's slurred words as he pulled the covers up to her shoulder. After Rebekah had gotten the intoxicated woman into a t-shirt and a pair of shorts, Luke had eased her over to the four-poster bed. He hoped she had at least changed the mattress in the years since it had been his bed; it had been getting uncomfortable when he left for college.

Constance's bedroom was much the same as Luke remembered; before he left for college, it had been his bedroom. The bed sat in the northeast corner of the bedroom, its headboard against the north wall, its side as flush as possible against the east. The desk, bureau, and black vinyl couch were all in the same positions they'd been back then; only the clutter and the newer-but-peeling wallpaper were different. At the foot of the bed sat a dresser with a large oval mirror attached to the dresser at its narrow end. A crack ran through the dark wood holding the mirror, a crack that Luke remembered well; it had happened when James had shoved Constance against the dresser, the night his grandmother had made him her emissary.

"Matthew," Constance said, her slurred voice hesitating, "you're a good son." Luke finished tucking her in. He'd laid her down on her side, to make sure she wouldn't choke if she threw up. Rebekah had found a plastic washbasin in the bathroom, under the counter in there; he placed it on the floor, next to Constance's head, so that if she did throw up again, it would at least be easy to clean up.

"I'm not Matthew, Mother," Luke said as he picked up a quilt from the couch behind him. "I'm Luke."

"Oh," she said, "Luke." She made a grumbling noise that Luke could not decipher. He stood back, in case she was about to throw up again. When she didn't, he decided it was safe and placed the quilt behind her on the bed, to keep her from rolling onto her back when she passed out, which he hoped she would do soon. After a moment of thought, while Constance mumbled and groaned more things Luke couldn't make out, he decided to move her back on the bed a little bit and put another rolled-up quilt in front of her, to keep her from rolling forward and landing on the floor. The quilts he used were both familiar to him; his grandmother had made them, long ago. He remembered watching her put up the quilting frames and move deftly around and below the stretched cloth, sewing by hand as quickly and adroitly as a spider weaving a web.

An ache filled his heart at the thought of his grandmother. *Maybe if the quilts are still clean tomorrow, I'll try to take one home with me.* "There," he said. "You should be okay now." He headed for the door.

"Luke," Constance said, her voice wavering but not quite as slurred as before.

"What?"

"James - he really is dead, ain't he?"

Luke stopped, his hand on the doorknob, and lowered his head. Had she forgotten in her stupor? Or merely been in denial all along? "Yes, Mother," he said softly, "James really is dead."

"Oh, oh God," she said, and began crying softly against the pillow. Luke stepped back from the door, hoping to console her somehow, but she put out a hand to stop him before he got close to the bed. "I'm okay. I'm okay. He just — you took care of it all, didn't you? You, you took care of him, right?"

Luke sighed, for what felt like the millionth time since coming back to Riverton. "Yes, Mother, I did. It's all taken care of."

"You should have," Constance said through her sniffles, surprising Luke. "It's what's right. When I, when I go away - Matthew'll — he'll take care of me. Like you did for James."

Her words confused Luke. Did she think he wouldn't have done the same for her, if Matthew or Rebekah or Werner didn't? "That's not fair, Mother. I'd do the same for you as I did for James, if I needed to."

"'S'all right, Luke, 'sokay. Matthew's *my* son. You were always more his than mine. *Theirs*, really ...."

"What the hell are you talking about?" Luke felt his left hand clenching and unclenching, unbidden; he held it behind his back in the hope she wouldn't notice before it relaxed.

Constance turned slightly, so she could look directly at Luke, leaning back on the quilt he'd placed behind her. Her eyes were unsteady, barely focusing; like her voice, they were filled with a swirl of emotions he could not completely sort out. "You, you're *his* son, Luke. So much like him — knew it when you were born. You was his more than, than you'd ever be mine. You had his look in yo' little baby eyes."

She waved a hand in a lazy, haphazard circle as she tried to explain. "Look that says, you're only, only here … until you go. 'Til the winds of whims took you somewhere else. *His*, not *mine* …."

Confused, Luke sat down on the couch. "Mother, you're not making any sense. You're drunk; you need to sleep it off and —"

"*I'm* not - not that drunk. Yo' grandma saw it too, she said it, when you was born. She said - I 'member it, I was there - she said 'this boy ain't meant for here'." Constance's drunken slur suddenly took on a tone Luke couldn't define, something somewhere between contempt and resentment; maybe envy? "Like you was so special, like the rest of us — like we was meant to be here, in this shithole town, but you, she looked at you like, like, like you was better than Riverton."

Luke didn't know whether to be more shocked at the current of anger in his mother's voice or the fact that she had actually cursed – or the revelation of her resentment against him.

"An' James, that bastard. He felt same way she did.
First time he saw you at tha hospital—"

"He came to the hospital after I was born?" Luke
interjected, his left hand clenched tighter than he could
remember it ever being. "You couldn't have had him sign
my bloody birth certificate while he was there?" That blank,
empty line on the certificate had been a sore spot for Luke,
long ago, but he'd figured himself over it. At least, he had,
until the words leapt out of his mouth.

"Ha," Constance sniffed, wiping her eye with one
unsteady hand, "that was both of them. He didn't wan' me
comin' after him for money. And *she* didn't wan' him havin'
no legal claim on you—" She belched loudly; Luke covered
his mouth and nose with his hand to avoid the boozy fumes.
"Naw, they agreed on that. Fo' different reasons, though."

"Okay," Luke said, standing up. "You are *really* drunk,
and making very little sense. Get some sleep and we'll—"

"Shut up!"

Stunned by the command, Luke complied and sat back
down. He regarded his mother warily; there was definite
anger in her voice, in her eyes, in the cruel twist of her
mouth. "Both of them, they thought, they thought ... you
were so goddamn special. Why? What was so good about
you? Oh, they tried to be as nice to Rebekah and Matthew,
but you, you was both their favorites. Hell, they cared 'bout
you more than they did me, an' I *made* you ...."

Luke hated the slow burn in his chest, the coldness in his
voice when he spoke. He hated them, but his mother was
pushing all of his buttons. If she wanted his anger, it didn't
seem unreasonable to give it to her – except it was. He knew

it, and struggled to keep his temper in check. "At least I was *someone's* favorite," he said, the calm, cold, measured tone of his words an odd reflection of the fire growing inside him. "I sure as hell wasn't *yours.*"

"Oh, *screw* you," Constance retorted, her tears flowing more freely. "Did you ever have to ask James for anything? No, you didn', he jus' sent you money. *I* had to beg him when I, when I needed money from him. *I had to beg* for what he just *threw* at you! And you didn't even *want* it!"

Luke balled his left hand into a fist, unballed it, balled again. "That was his choice, *Mother*, not mine."

"But you sure as hell didn't try to stop him! You never stood up and said, 'hey, why don't you send some money to 'Bekah? Why don't you give Matthew some money?' Nope, you just let him do what he wanted!"

"Why didn't you?" Clench, unclench, clench.

"*I did!* And you, you know what he told me? He said they had *me* and they didn't need his help as much you did! But he wasn't here! He didn't know what they needed! He didn't know what *I* needed!"

"And you are taking that out on me for what reason, exactly?"

"Because you're *his!* You're not my son! I gave birth to you, but you're not mine, not really. You're *his* and *hers* - that spiteful old bitch."

Luke's blood thundered in his ears, but his voice dropped another ten degrees. "She owned this house. You didn't like it, why didn't you leave?"

Constance shot up into a sitting position, her hands moving swiftly if drunkenly between pointing at him when she spoke of James and pointing at herself the rest fo the time. "Because I waited for *him*, like a goddamn fool! I waited for him, and every time we talked, he said he was leaving his wife *soon*! He'll move back to town *soon*! He'll quit truck driving *soon*! And I waited *years*, Luke, my whole goddamn *life* wasted waiting for that man! And *she* never let me forget it! She hated him, but she loved you and Rebekah, she doted on you two and left Matthew out in the cold!"

"Wait, Rebekah?"

"You don't even see it! She *groomed* Rebekah, she raised her up to be *just like her*, and she is, she'll be running this family and the church and everything 'fore I'm even in the grave! She never even gave *me* a chance!"

Even in his anger, Luke had to admit that her words rang true. Rebekah was always the best at keeping in touch with relatives, was good with people, had the most easygoing manner. He hadn't really considered it before, but now that Constance mentioned it, he could easily imagine Rebekah taking his grandmother's place in the family. "That seems about right to me."

Constance's finger jabbed viciously at Luke. "You *would* take her side! I wish you'd let Matthew kill James when he had the chance! Or your grandmother had shot him when she said she would. That's how much she didn't care about me, right there!

"I'm not – I don't understand." Luke didn't know what to feel or how to feel here. His mother had never opened up

169

like this before, never been so straightforward and honest – and never said such terrible, painful things.

"Goddammit, Luke, you don't even *talk* like me. *You* were why she threatened to shoot James! Not for, for of all the times he cheated on *me*, not for all the times he fought and pushed and shoved *me*, not for how he treated the rest of *my*, my children - no, not for *me*. When she finally decided she'd had enough of his shit was when he threatened, threatened *you*." Constance curled up on the bed, her body wracked with heaving sobs. "Y'all don't care about me, none of y'all ever did. Except Matthew. Rebekah was *hers*, you were *his*, Matthew was the only one that stuck by *me*."

Luke stood up. Confronted with the sight of the drunken woman before him, he felt his anger begin to slowly ebb. She looked too pathetic to be angry at her. He reached out, took her hand, and lifted it level with his chest. "Mother…" he began.

Quick as a striking snake, Constance whipped her hand back from his. *"Fuck you!"* she yelled, reaching for the washbasin he'd thoughtfully placed beside the bed and throwing it at him. *"You're not my* real *son!"*

Luke batted it aside even faster than she had snatched her hand back from him. As he did, he felt the anger in him rise, higher than before. Then it levelled out, his mind colder than ice but his rage burning hotter than hell.

"Enough!" he bellowed, loud enough, his voice deep enough, that the windows, rattled with the force of it. Beneath his feet, a million miles from the fire in his chest, he felt the floorboards vibrate as his voice resounded in the small room. Through the open bedroom door, Luke heard

Rebekah's voice, all the way from the living room. "Oh, *shit*."

Luke hated raising his voice. Luke hated losing his temper, knew that hate only fed into the rage and made it worse, but he hadn't been able to stop it; Constance was throwing it all out there now, and the torrent of her hurt pulled him along for the ride, ripped away skin from wounds he'd long thought healed, pulled out a hate-filled hurt of his own that he'd locked away.

On the bed, Constance shrank back from him, the anger and bitterness that had contorted her features fleeing as his voice rolled over her, leaving only fear in their wake. Luke hated the tears and scared look on her pitiful face, too.

"You're *drunk*. Sleep it off. *Now*. We'll talk tomorrow, before I leave." Without waiting for her reply, Luke left the bedroom, slamming the door as hard as he could behind him. It wouldn't help her sleep, he knew, but his anger demanded expression.

As he stormed down the hall, he heard a door open behind him, to his left: the door to Matthew's room. He knew Matthew would be peeking out, wondering what had happened. Luke stopped, but didn't turn around.

"Close. Your. *Fucking*. Door," he growled.

The door closed with a soft *snick*.

Luke went into the living room, where Alexis and Sierra were sitting on the couch. Rebekah sat in a chair from the dining room, across the coffee table from the other two women, a deck of cards in her hand. "Luke," Rebekah said, "what hap —"

Luke didn't even slow down. "Is Werner still outside?"

"Naw, he left. What—"

"Going outside," Luke called from the dining room. "Need to make a phone call."

"Want us to—"

"I need to be alone for it," he called from the kitchen door, then regretted his curtness to his sisters and wife. He chided himself for snapping at them; they'd done nothing wrong. "Please," he added, and stepped into the garage.

****

Outside, the light autumn rain had turned into a sudden storm. Luke liked it; it suited his mood perfectly as he dialed his phone.

"Hey, what's up, bro?"

"Christopher." Luke pulled out his pack of cigarettes.

"Uh oh, what's going on?"

"You need to tell me what happened. Why my grandmother threatened to shoot James."

"Hey, I told you to ask Con-"

"She's a drunken, sobbing mess right now. That leaves you, since I assume you heard it from the horse's mouth, so to speak."

"Okay." Christopher paused. "So, do you want to meet up later, or-"

"Now is good." He had to hold the phone with his shoulder as he lit the cigarette.

"I ain't so sure, Luke. I think you need to—"

"Christopher."

"What?"

"I said *now*."

A dry, bitter chuckle came through the phone to Luke's ears. Even deprived of mirth, it still sounded like James' chuckle. "Guess he gave all his boys temper problems, huh?"

"Christopher."

"All right, all right, damn. Chill out a little, bro, it ain't that serious."

Luke took a drag of his cigarette. "What did I say that sounded like 'waste my time'?"

The smile left Christopher's voice. "Fine. About a year before you married Sierra, James was livin' with Constance and your grandmother out there. That was before Matthew moved back from Houston."

"I remember. Continue."

"James and Constance had a fight because James was cheatin' on her with Momma, and James decided he wanted to leave. So he packed a suitcase up and everything. He was walking out the house, and she was following behind him, telling him Momma wouldn't take his cheatin' ass either, and Phoebe sure as shit didn't want him again, so he didn't have nowhere else to go. That was when they walked into the living room, and there was yo' grandmomma, sittin' in her chair, readin' the newspaper like it wasn't two grown-ass people shoutin' at each other ten feet away.

"Well, James said since nobody in Riverton wanted him, he'd have fly out to Seattle and live with you instead. That was when yo' grandmomma spoke up."

Christopher paused; Luke could hear him lighting a cigarette of his own. "She told him to stay away from you, that you had outgrown him and Riverton and you didn't need his bullshit on yo' doorstep. That's what James said she said, when he told me what happened.

"And Constance, she laughed at him when yo' grandmomma said that, laughed and told him his ass wasn' goin' nowhere, that nobody wanted him and he'd die alone and unwanted, just all kinds of mean shit."

"Yeah," Luke said, taking another drag, "she's got a talent for that sometimes."

"She got a habit of bein' right sometimes too then, 'cause that's pretty much what happened."

"Keep going. Please."

"Anyway," Christopher continued, "that just made him madder, and he decided right then he was going to call and get a plane ticket and go out to Seattle.

"But yo' grandmomma, she said that if he ever tried that, or she ever heard he was even thinkin' hard about it, she was going to shoot him where he stood and use his body to fertilize her rosebushes."

"Well," Luke said as he lit another cigarette, "she did love her rosebushes."

"More'n she loved him, for damn sure. But James, so he said, was too mad to listen to her. He picked up the phone book, flipped through it right quick, with Constance yellin' at him the whole time, picked up the phone, and he said as soon as the words 'I need to book a flight' came out his mouth, he heard a *click* noise. He looked up at yo' grandmomma, and she had that ol' pistol she kept beside her chair in her hands, that, what was it?"

"Don't matter. Keep going." Luke knew exactly what he was talking about: a revolver that she always kept oiled, loaded, and in perfect working condition. Though it was over a hundred years old, older than her by over twenty years, Luke had no doubt it would have fired as well as the day it was new. He wondered what had become of it after her death; Constance disdained guns and his uncles had their own weapons.

"So, she had that ol' pistol in her hands, aimed at him, cocked, locked, and loaded. He said he hung up the phone and left the house without another word, and Constance was too shocked to say shit. He ain't have no doubt she woulda shot him if he'd tried to buy that ticket."

"Heh," Luke said, smiling weakly to himself. "Grandma don't shiv."

"What?"

"Nothing. Keep going."

"Well, you know the rest. Spent two months livin' in a cheap motel until he talked Momma inta lettin' him live here. Then they got married, and, well, you know the rest. Hell, you helped write the end to that story."

"Yeah. I did, I guess." He heard the sadness creep into his voice. He believed the story; it really did sound like something she would have done. But would it really have been an act of love for Luke? How could murdering someone's father be the act of a loving person?

"Hey, don't judge her too harsh, all right? She just didn't want him messin' up yo' life like he did everybody else's. She really loved you, from what I know."

"I know," Luke replied, leaning against the wall. He felt tears burning his eyes, and didn't know if they were from the subsiding rage and frustration with his mother or love and confusion about his grandmother – and he supposed it didn't matter.

"You okay?"

"I gotta go. Sierra's here, I need to—"

"She is? Bring her by before you leave, bro! I ain't seen her in a minute. Ain't likely to see *you* again for minute, either."

Luke ground his cigarette out on the concrete floor. "All right, I will. Look, I'm sorry for being so rude earlier. It's been …" Luke sighed again, his breath hitching. "It's been a pretty fucking hard day."

"You're my brother, man. Shit happens, I dig. Check you tomorrow." Christopher hung up

Luke slumped down against the wall, knees bent and raised in front of him. Had anyone asked him, he would have said he was completely emotionally drained, hollowed of all ability to feel anything, but the tears came anyway, flowing freely, wet and hot on his cheeks as he leaned his forehead against his knees. His grandmother, Constance, James — they all danced in his head, all insanely complex threads in the sad tapestry of his past. Suddenly, the house, the garage, Riverton, all of Mississippi, all of it felt irreparably foreign to him, abruptly alien, unfamiliar, strange. *I just want to go home*, he thought, tasting salt on his lips as he cried. *But where is that? Where do I really belong?*

When he felt Sierra's arms slide around him, Luke knew he had his answer.

****

Rebekah and Alexis gave him curious glances as he stood up.

"Are you okay?" Rebekah asked, her brow furrowed, her hand soft but firm on his shoulder. Looking into her eyes, it was undeniable: the same concern, the same worry, the same quiet strength. And the beginnings of the same wisdom. He had no doubts now; Rebekah was definitely what Constance had viciously labeled her. Luke had never loved his sister more than he did in that moment.

"I'm fine," he told her, and gave her a tight hug. As he did, he noticed the purse on her arm, the keys in her hand. "You leaving?"

"Yeah. I gotta go pick the kids up from their dumb-ass daddy, and get Alexis home so she can pick Richie up."

Beside her, Alexis nodded. "It's almost 4. I'm old, it's getting late for me."

"Don't forget your wheelchair," Luke replied with a wan grin.

"Smartass," she replied, and gave him a tight hug. "I prob'ly won't see you before you leave tomorrow, so y'all travel safe. And keep in touch, this time. Sierra's got my number too, so y'all ain't got no excuses."

Luke gave her a kiss on the cheek as they separated, then waited for her to hug Sierra before he spoke again. "Thanks for everything, Alexis. I mean it, you've been - I couldn't have made it through this without you. I love you."

"Oh hell, you gettin' all mushy, it's time to go." She smiled as she walked towards Rebekah's car. "I love you too. You still a brat, though. Good seeing you, Sierra!"

"You too," Sierra replied, smiling warmly at Alexis.

"I gotta work tomorrow," Rebekah said, "got rent to pay, you know how that is." She embraced him again, then did the same with Sierra. "Good to see both of y'all. Maybe this year I'll make it out there to visit."

"I hope so," Sierra said.

Luke squeezed Sierra to his side. "We love you, sister mine," he said.

"Shit," Rebekah replied, "Alexis was right. It *is* time to go. I love y'all," she said, waving as she left the garage and went to her car. Sierra and Luke stayed inside the garage and watched her car pull away in the pouring rain.

After they were gone, Sierra turned to Luke. "Do you want to talk about it?" There was concern in her eyes and voice.

"Later," he said, entwining his fingers in hers. "I just – I have a lot of thinking to do."

"About what?" she asked, squeezing his hand.

"About James, about Mother, about Grandma, all of it. All of them. Maybe they're more complex than I ever thought, and I didn't realize it because – because I didn't want to." He kissed her cheek. "I'm really glad you're here."

"Me too," she said, leaning on his shoulder. "I'm sorry things with Constance – "

"Later, please," Luke said. Though he didn't want to think about it, his mind flashed on what she'd said in her drunken rant. *"Rebekah was hers, you were his."* Luke realized that, with him about to leave, and Rebekah already gone and probably not coming back until late, Matthew was the only one there to comfort her. She'd been absolutely correct. But how much of that isolation was self-imposed? How muchwas who they are versus who she is, and how much was her pushing them away? He felt the tears bite again. "I don't think I can handle – "

Luke's phone rang. He pulled it out of his pocket, glancing at the display. "Alexis?"

"Hey, Luke, don't leave the house yet. Have another smoke or something."

"What? Why?"

"I don't want you to scare her off. She'll probably run, she sees you coming."

"Huh ?"

"Go look," Alexis replied, and hung up.

Luke stepped out into the rain to see around the house, taking Sierra with him by forgetting to let go of her hand. "What's going on?" she asked, throwing her free hand over her hair.

Someone was standing in the cemetery, near the recently filled-in grave.

The rain had fortunately diminished to just a drizzle, and the day was still fairly bright. Luke could not distinguish the features of the person standing at his father's resting place, but even from that distance, he could make out their pale skin and blond hair.

Luke turned to Sierra. "That's Phoebe," he said.

Sierra frowned. "All alone, in a cemetery, in the rain … that's sad."

"That's Phoebe."

CHAPTER NINE

"I feel like I'm forgetting something. Are you sure that's everything?" Luke asked, looking around the hotel room, his brows knitting as he tried to figure out what he was forgetting.

"Well, it's definitely all *my* stuff. I didn't bring much," Sierra replied as she put her overnight bag by the door, next to Luke's carry-on bag. The room was cleaned out, all of their belongings gathered by the door except for Luke's suitcase, which sat open and nearly full on the bed.

"Hang on, I need to check the bathroom — oh! Would you see if you can fit some of my clothes in your bag? I need to leave room in the suitcase for couple of small quilts."

"Where are we getting a quilt?"

Luke emerged from the bathroom with his electric toothbrush and toothpaste. "Knew I was forgetting something." He tucked the dental care items into the side pocket of his suitcase. "There are still some of my grandmother's handmade quilts out at her house. I wanna take one or two back with us."

"Hm," Sierra said, as she packed a pair of Luke's pants into her bag.

Luke zipped the suitcase shut. "What?"

"You."

"What about me?" he asked, abandoning the suitcase to wrap his arms around Sierra's waist, pulling her close to him.

She kissed him on the cheek. "You still call it your grandmother's house. It's Constance's now."

"Oh, yeah. Well, it was when I grew up. It kinda always will be, to me."

Sierra ran the backs of her fingers along his cheek. "I know you loved her and had a lot of respect for her. But it sounded like she wasn't as saintly as you made her out to be."

Luke frowned. "She wasn't, I guess – no, I know." he said, a cloud in his features. "It's just hard to let go of her." But it wasn't really her that he had to let go of, and Luke knew that.

She kissed him again, a quick peck on the lips. "I know it is, baby. But it might help improve things between you and Constance. Shhhh," she said, placing a finger on his lips as he opened them to speak. "It might be too late to fix things between you two, but you owe it to your family to try."

"I know, you're right, I know. It's just hard," Luke replied. He hugged his wife tight, resting his head on her shoulder. Luke took comfort and strength in her encircling arms, the feel of her body against him, the certain knowledge that he was not alone.

"I know, I know," she said as she stroked the back of his head. "I'm not saying to forget about her, just try not to cling to ghosts so hard, you know? I know she was super-important to you, but don't let her ghost rule your life. Hers or your father's."

"I'll try," Luke said, stepping back from her. "I promise, I'll try. We should get going, though. Got a lot to do before we hit the road."

"Aye aye, Cap'n," Sierra replied with a smile. "Where all do we have to go?"

"We're going to visit the alive, the dead, and various points in-between."

****

As Luke approached the door, he saw a familiar old woman sitting on her porch, watching him warily from her position across the parking lot. He couldn't fault her for being wary, after what happened the last time he'd visited. Behind him, Sierra sat in the car, reading a book; he'd asked to do this alone and she concurred, after he'd filled in some backstory for her. He waved to the old woman, smiling at her. She raised a cautious hand, more in simple acknowledgement than in reply.

Anxiety filled him as he raised his hand to knock on the door. He pushed it down and knocked anyway.

There was no reply.

He knocked again, noticing a bit of chill in the air.

This time, there was an answer. "Who is it?"

"It's Luke, Phoebe."

"Fuck." she replied, opening the door. It swung open only two inches before the chain on the back stopped it. Phoebe peeked out at him through the gap. "What the fuck you want, asshole?"

Though it had been only three days since he'd last seen her, Phoebe had aged years. What Luke could see of her pale face was worn and haggard, her skin sallow and loose upon her skull. Her eyes were bloodshot and bagged. She held a black terrycloth robe closed at her collarbone. Her breath reeked of weed and cigarettes, mixed with alcohol — a *lot* of alcohol and a *lot* of weed, Luke thought. She smelled the way Luke imagined that Tim's house would after a long weekend.

Luke decided to keep that sentiment to himself; he was trying to be nice today. "Phoebe, I just wanted to talk."

"So talk."

Luke caught the sigh in his chest and stifled it. "James is dead, Phoebe. Dead and buried. I buried him myself. Letitia is dead, too. Why can't we –"

From the stairs behind Phoebe, a man's voice echoed down the stairs. It sounded either sleepy or intoxicated; Luke wasn't sure which and didn't want to know. "Where my babygirl at? Daddy's lonely up here!"

"I'll be up in a minute! Calm yo' ass down!" Phoebe yelled back. "Just met me yesterday, old muthafucka, you don't own me," she muttered, then turned back to Luke. "What was you sayin'?"

Luke considered just leaving and coming back another time. But he didn't know when he would be back in Riverton; given the funeral-related tightness of his budget, it was probably going to be a while. He decided to press on and try to resolve things now. "I was saying James is dead. Letitia's dead. You and I, we're still alive. Why can't we make peace? Why can't we be - well, maybe not friends, exactly, but *family*? Not at each other's throats all the time? Why can't we talk about James and help each other deal with what he did to both of us?"

Phoebe sighed, wetness visible in her eyes before she dropped her head. "You don't understand, Luke, you never did. You never knew my momma, what that man took away from me. You helped him do it, you and Constance and fuckin' Billie, all them and they fuckin' kids, y'all don't ever understand."

"It's the past, Phoebe, we *can* let it go. Why can't we at least try and maybe help each other deal?"

"*You* can, Luke," she snapped, raising her head. The anger in her eyes was familiar to him, but hadn't quite crept into her voice yet. "*You* can. You got *everything* from him. You don't know what it's like to get nothing *from* and lose everything *to* him."

"Then tell me what it was like, please! You don't have to-"

"Shut up, Luke, I ain't done yet!" Phoebe's voice was rising. "You got to get his body and have a pretty little funeral and put him in the ground! *I* couldn't do that! *You* got to bury his whole body, Luke! *I* got nothing! Never found her body! Don't tell me you fuckin' *understand*, Luke, you can't. You got *everything*, Luke, I *know* you did! I can even see yo' pretty little white wife sittin' in the car! I had everything. *He* took it all away, and *you* helped. Don't tell yo' *victim* you understand what you did to her!"

Luke sighed; he just couldn't hold it in. "Phoebe, I was a kid, just like you. An innocent person, just like you."

"Bullshit," Phoebe sneered. "You was *born* of sin; you wasn't *never* innocent."

Luke sighed again and shrugged. "I had to try."

"No, you didn't. You coulda just went ahead and gone to Hell wit' yo' daddy, for what I cared."

"That's not fair."

"So? Get the fuck away from my house."

Luke turned from the door, intending to step away, but before he could, the words burst from his mouth. "If you ever change your mind, let me know, Phoebe. It doesn't have to be this way."

To Luke's surprise, Phoebe started crying. He watched the first tears, fat and shiny, roll down her cheeks as her head tilted downwards, hiding her eyes from him.

The words came from her lips in a near-whisper. "Yes, it does, Luke. Yes, it does."

The door closed softly between them.

****

Another door swung wide open.

"Little bro, wassup!" Christopher stood in the open door, grinning from ear to ear. He reached out and pulled Luke into a tight hug, making Luke grunt. "Oh, and you got Miss Sierra with you, huh?" He quickly released Luke and gave Sierra a warm hug. "How you doin', sis-in-law? Keepin' my little brother outta trouble?"

"Trying to," Sierra said, smiling, as Christopher let her go and led them both into Billie's house. "How are you doing?"

"Oh, I'm good, I'm good," he replied. With a gesture, he waved them into the living room while he went into the kitchen. "Can I get y'all some water? Juice? Beer?"

"We're good, but I thought you couldn't drink?" Luke said. He sat on the plastic-covered couch gently, trying not to make much noise, and failed miserably. Beside him, Sierra sat down gingerly and managed not to make any sound at all. "Show off," Luke whispered to her.

"It's an art," she replied with a wink.

"I don't," Christopher replied from the kitchen, "but I keep some around for guests." He walked into the living room with a big glass of water and sat down in Billie's chair. "So I'm guessin' you had an interestin' weekend, huh?"

Luke rolled his eyes. "Oh, it was a hoot and a holler! You shoulda been there."

A cloud crossed Christopher's features. Then it was gone, and his wide smile returned so quickly it might never have left. "Nah," he said, "wasn't my type of party. Plus I had to work. They're makin' me shift supervisor, starting next week. It's an extra $3 an hour, which puts me at close $20, finally."

"Nice! But what about the extra work?"

"Hell, I was already doin' that. The supervisor we got now is a fuckin' idiot," Christopher said, then looked at Sierra. "Pardon my French."

"Oh, I speak French," Sierra replied with a grin of her own.

"Ha! I like that attitude! Hey, bro, you gotta keep her, all right?"

"The question isn't me keeping her, the question is *her* keeping *me*."

Christopher laughed again, loud and hearty. "Guess you got a little smarter since you left here, huh?

"Little bit, yeah. " Luke looked around. "Where's Billie?"

"Aw, she had a lunch date with some dude from her work."

"A date? Really?"

"Yeah, he quit workin' there a couple weeks ago, figured it was safe to ask her out now, so, she went, but she had to wear sunglasses after yesterday."

Luke raised his eyebrow.

"It's so cute when you do that," Sierra said, making Christopher laugh again. "What? It *is* cute." Christopher laughed harder, while Luke blushed. "Now when you do *that*, it's just *adorable*. It makes your freckles stand out more." Luke put his face in his hands. Christopher roared with laughter.

When he calmed down, he wiped tears away from his eyes. "Oh shoot, you two are freakin' funny together. Come on," he said as he stood up, "come smoke with me." When he saw Sierra get up as well, he asked, "You smoke too?"

"Not much," she replied, "but it goes along with speaking French."

On the porch, Luke sat down, while Christopher offered his chair to Sierra. Luke lit his and Sierra's cigarettes while Christopher lit his from a match. "So what happened yesterday?" Luke asked.

"Oh, Billie went out with Constance while I guess the funeral was goin' on. I don't know where they went, but she came back four sheets to the wind."

"Poor Werner," Luke said, shaking his head. "He had to deal with both of them drunk."

"I put her in bed when she got back, and she slept till this morning. Momma don't get drunk much, so she had a hell of a hangover, but she wanted to keep that date."

"Guess she's movin' on from James," Sierra said.

"Yeah," Christopher replied with a slight frown. "I guess she is."

"What about you?" Luke inquired.

Christopher's brows knit. "I don't know, bro. It's just - I don't know. I'll try."

"I seem to be hearing that a lot today," Sierra said.

Christopher raised his eyebrow at her.

"Oh my God, you *both* do it!" she said, laughing.

"Something else we got from him, I guess," Luke said.

"Yeah, I guess so." Christopher looked down, his features dark. "But, you know what?"

"What?"

"When I talk to those kids at church, the ones that used to be in gangs? I talk about him. I talk about what it was like for me, growin' up without my dad, and then when he was around, never hearin' he loved me or cared about me. And a lot of those kids, they grew up without their dads too, or their dad was abusive or mean, they never felt loved either. So when I talk about James, they know I understand what their lives were like."

"That's good, yeah?"

"Yeah, it is. They trust me, and they open up to me, because I *understand*. Because I know that pain. They know I get it when they talk. And I think that's ..." He paused for a deep, hitching breath. "I think that's all they ever really needed, was just somebody that *understood*. And I get to be that somebody. I think that's what the Lord wants me to do, is be that somebody for them. I don't know I'll ever forgive James for what he put me and Momma through, but at least this way, some good comes out of it. Some kids that might never have had a chance at life get one."

"I think that's great," Sierra said. "You found a way to use your pain to help others."

"Yeah," he replied, smiling weakly. "I guess I did."

"Christopher," Luke said. He stood from the chair and moved forward until he was directly in front of his brother. "I think James did the best he could with what he had, but he just didn't have much. He wasn't that smart, never had much money, and fucked up – a lot – but he tried."

"That's what you think, huh?"

"I do," Luke said, staring his brother directly in the eye. "He was just human, just a man. Just like any of us. And I think he'd be proud of you."

A challenging look appeared on Christopher's face. "What makes you think that? He never talked about his feelings, he didn't like to get 'mushy', remember? And he hadn't talked to you for years."

Luke put a hand on Christopher's shoulder and squeezed it gently, without breaking eye contact. "Because you're a good man, a better man than he was, and *I'm* proud of you."

Christopher's lips wavered as his tried to speak, but no words came out. Instead, he pulled Luke towards him in a tight hug.

"Thank you, bro," Christopher said, releasing Luke and stepping back. "It's good to hear that sometimes."

"'S all good, bro," Luke said.

"Luke," Sierra said, tapping her watch. "Hate to break this up, but they're not gonna hold the plane just for us, and you still have to go see Constance."

"Right, right," Christopher said, giving Luke another hug. "And it was good to see you too," he added as he gave Sierra a hug. "Be in touch more, okay?"

"Okay," she replied. "I think Rebekah is going to come try to visit next year; maybe you should try to come with her, Mister Moneybags."

"If alimony and child support don't leave me broke," Christopher said, smiling. "Let me go do some laundry 'fore Momma gets back."

As they walked back to the car, Sierra asked Luke, "What made you say that?"

Luke opened her door and watched as she slid into the passenger seat. "It was what you said about using your own pain to help others."

"It was?" she continued when he opened the driver-side door. "How did your own pain tell you to do that to help others?"

Luke started the car. "You think Constance *or* James ever told me they were proud of me?"

****

"Leave the flowers," Luke said to Sierra, who was reaching into the backseat.

"I'm not reaching for those," she replied, digging in her overnight bag. "I brought a present for Matthew — some of those oil paints. You said he paints, right?"

"Yeah, but don't expect to talk to him."

"We'll just leave them by his door — well, hello there!" Sierra said. Bingo had trotted up to her, tail wagging furiously and tongue flicking out to lick her hand. "You're not too good a guard dog, but you sure are friendly, aren't you?" Bingo woofed in apparent agreement.

"Maybe to *you*," Luke said, unlocking the back door with his key. "He barked his bloody head off at me last week."

Sierra followed him inside. "Maybe I smell better," she joked.

The living room, to Luke's surprise, was empty. "Hello?" he called out.

"I'm in the back!" Constance yelled back.

Luke took Sierra's hand. "Penultimate stop," he said. "Let's get this over with."

In the bedroom, Constance was still in bed, sitting up, leaning against a mound of pillows. She did appear to have gotten up and changed clothes, Luke saw, and from the faint scent of soap he detected, he guessed she had also taken a shower before returning to bed. As he entered the room, he couldn't help glancing at the plastic washbasin she'd thrown at him the day before, still in the corner near the dresser, where it had fallen after he'd knocked it out of the air.

"Well hey, Sierra," Constance croaked. Her voice was rough and raspy. From the shiny spot on the floor, Luke figured she'd thrown up at least once more after his departure. Hopefully that had helped get the booze out of her system.

"Hey Constance," Sierra replied, her voice uncertain. "How are you feeling?"

"Oh, not too good," the older woman replied with a sheepish smile. "I guess I overdid it yesterday. How y'all doin'?"

Sierra sat down on the couch. As they chatted, Luke looked around and saw the quilts he'd used to prop her up laying on the couch. He pulled them up and checked them; they appeared to have been spared her sickness. He was glad of that; he didn't have time to wash them and he didn't want his clothes smelling of her unwillingly-evicted food.

194

"Luke, you bein' mighty quiet," Constance said.

"Oh," Luke said, startled by her sudden focus on him. "I wanted to ask if we could take these quilts back with us."

Constance grimaced, then smiled again. "You might as well, we got plenty." She looked at the clock beside her bed. "Y'all need to get going soon. Sierra, why don't you go put those in y'all's suitcase? Luke'll be out in a minute."

Sierra looked at Luke, who nodded, then rose, quilts in hand. "All right, Constance. I hope you feel better soon."

"Oh, I'm sure I will," Constance replied, smiling.

"I'll be out soon," Luke said, giving Sierra a kiss on the cheek.

"Okay," she said, loud enough for Constance to hear, then whispered, "Be nice."

"No promises," Luke replied, and closed the door halfway behind her. When he turned back to Constance, her smile was gone, replaced with an inscrutably placid expression.

"Luke ..."

"Mother," he replied, taking a seat on the couch.

"Luke, I was really drunk yesterday, wasn't I?"

"Yeah, you were. I guess you and Billie really put a few down."

She smiled, briefly. "Too many, way too many. Thank you for puttin' me in bed. I musta been a mess."

"Yeah, well, you do for family." Luke wondered what her point was, what she was *really* trying to say.

"Yeah, you do."

A silence hung between them.

"I was really drunk," she repeated. "I don't remember anything that happened after the VFW. I don't even remember takin' Billie home."

Luke stared at her in disbelief.

"I know we *must* have took her home, but for the life of me, I can't remember. I don't even remember gettin' back into Werner's truck." Luke watched her look at everything in the room as she spoke: the desk under the window closest to her, the air conditioner, the dresser, the bureau, the doors. Everything except *him*. "Rebekah told me this mornin', before she left for work, Sierra and Alexis were here when I got home, but I don't even remember *seein'* them." Her hands, held together in her lap, clenched and unclenched, over and over. "I don't remember *nothin'* after the VFW, 'til I woke up here this mornin'. But I woke up, so I guess nothin' too bad happened, right?"

"Well, that depends on what you call 'too bad,'" Luke said, feeling incensed at her obvious lie. "First," he continued, counting on his fingers, "you —"

"*Luke.*"

She was definitely looking at him now, her tired eyes red-rimmed and pleading.

Be nice.

"What?" he replied.

"*Nothing happened* — right?" Her smile was weak and tinged with desperation.

Luke wanted to tell her what had happened. Luke wanted, badly, to have the conversation about James and his grandmother that he and Constance never had. Luke wanted to bring it out, in sobriety and daylight, and talk about it, deal with it.

But clearly, Constance did not. Whatever her reasons – embarrassment, shame, fear, whatever – she didn't want to talk about it. Looking into her eyes, Luke saw that she wanted desperately not to talk about it. She wanted all that truth to stay buried, *needed* it to stay buried, and even the reasons why she needed it would stay buried as well.

Be nice.

"Yes, *Mother*," he said, getting to his feet. "Nothing happened."

"Good," she said, visibly relaxing as she leaned back on the pillows. "Come give me a hug. When y'all comin' back?"

"I don't know," he said as they embraced, more formally than warmly. "I'm gonna need to work extra to make up for this trip, and we're gonna be really tight for a while, after paying for the funeral. We'll see, I guess."

"All right, then," Constance replied. She settled back onto the pillows. "What's that?" she asked, pointing at a paper bag Sierra had left on the couch.

"Oh - those are oil paints Sierra brought for Matthew."

"That was nice of her! She's sweet. I'll give 'em to him later, he's asleep right now."

"Okay," Luke said. "We need to get on the road, though."

"Yeah, y'all do." Constance closed her eyes. "You drive safe and don't drive too fast, all right?"

"I won't," Luke said, moving towards the door.

"Take care of yourself, Luke."

"You too, Mother."

Luke closed the door on his way out.

****

"Last stop, I promise."

"Don't take long," Sierra said. "We're gonna be cutting it a little closer than I like as it is."

"You're not coming?"

"No. I love you and all," She kissed his cheek. "But it kinda weirds me out when you talk to dead people."

"All right, be right back," Luke said as he closed the car door.

The plastic around the roses crinkled as he walked through the cemetery, joining the crunch of leaves under his feet. Luke was assured that he was the noisiest person present, at least. A squirrel leapt out of his way, a scavenged pecan held in its mouth.

Finally, he came to her grave. He bent down to put the rose bouquet on the stone, then stood, his hands in his pockets.

"Hello Grandma," he said. A chilly breeze rose as he spoke. "Hmm, getting cold out here. Well, October-in-Mississippi cold, not Seattle cold.

"I did what I came here to do, I guess. I paid for James' funeral, I got him buried and everything. He's in the hands of whoever takes care of souls, if anybody. I don't know. You do, one way or another, but you weren't exactly known for giving up secrets in life, and you haven't been any different in death."

From the safety of a tree branch, the squirrel chattered at him.

"Christopher told me what you did, Grandma. Don't think any less of him for telling tales out of school; he just did what I asked him to do. I guess I have a forceful personality sometimes. Probably got that from you. Anyway, he told me. I don't know how to feel about it. I wish you and I could have talked about it before you died.

"I think you were protecting me, and really, I wouldn't have wanted to deal with James coming out to Seattle. It would have been pretty awkward. I don't know if that was the right way to go about it. Maybe if you hadn't, him and Constance could have worked things out. Maybe he and I could have, if he'd still been living here, or could have if he'd come to Seattle. I don't know. It could have gone so many different ways. I guess I'll never know, because it only went one way in the end, didn't it?"

Wind whispering between headstones was the only reply.

"I've been thinking some, the past few days, about parents and children. I've been told, though I have agreed that the conversation never happened, that you favored Rebekah and I over Matthew and your own daughter. Looking back, I can see some truth in that. And I think you were right; Rebekah has qualities Constance doesn't, and I think those qualities will eventually make her a better replacement for you. Matthew never talks to anyone but Constance, so I don't see him ever stepping up either. I know you were doing what you thought was best; I could never bring the family together the way you could. Rebekah can.

"But I'm left wondering some things. I know you probably did what you thought best, in paying more attention to Rebekah and I. But I have to wonder if you could have achieved the same goals with a little less attention. If maybe you could have helped us, taught us, shaped us without hurting Constance? But then I also have to wonder: is that really what happened, or did Constance just see it that way? Did she *feel* you were biased towards us, and in her reactions to that, end up driving you to be so?

Even if your actions hurt Constance, though, it was up to her, I suppose, not to take it out on her own children."

The squirrel chattered impatiently and scampered onto another branch.

"What you saw in Rebekah and I ... was Constance ever ... did she ever have those qualities, and abandoned them when she felt you'd given up on her? Or did she just never have them? If she hadn't felt you'd given up on her, regardless of whether or not you actually did, would she have not pulled back so much from Rebekah and I to focus on Matthew? Would all of us have turned out differently, if only you'd given Constance more attention? Would she, stronger for your attention and endorsement, been strong enough to leave James once and for all earlier? Would I have even been born if that had happened? Or would I have been born into a more *normal* family?

"Too many questions, too many possibilities. Too many choices made to look back and second-guess them now. I don't know what could have been. Nobody does. We have to deal with what *is*. And that's ... this. This situation. This life.

"None of us were perfect, Grandma. Constance, Billie, Phoebe, James, Christopher, Matthew, Rebekah, Alexis, we're all flawed. We all made mistakes. Even you. Hell, some of us are still making them. But you know what?"

Nothing answered. In the silence, another squirrel roamed through the leaves.

"Grandma, all of us — we did the best we could with what we had. *Especially* you. Because we're human, all of us, dead or alive, we're all only human. And that's all we can ever do."

He wiped his eyes.

"I should go," he told the breeze. "I'm going to have to drive fast and watch out for cops as is. I just—thank you for your love, and your attention, and your care. I wouldn't be who I am without you. I love you, Grandma."

He looked to the southern end of the cemetery, to the oblong patch where no grass was growing – though he knew it would return – and few leaves rested. "Goodbye, James Jackson. You helped shape me, too, in your way. I love you. And I forgive you."

He crouched down and kissed the tips of his fingers, then touched them to his grandmother's red marble tombstone. "Goodbye, Mary Alicia Hope Johnson. I love you."

Luke walked back to the car, back to his waiting wife, and began the long trip home.

11/12/2012 – 2/7/2013

The Burial

ACKNOWLEDGEMENTS

They say that it takes a village to raise a child, which I believe to be correct. They didn't say that it also takes a village to write and self-publish a book, which I believe to be a gross oversight.

First, a big thank you to the reader(s) of my Twilight Greyce blog (www.twilightgreyce.wordpress.com), who were patient and stuck with me as I wrote and posted each new chapter of *The Burial*, plus details of the new writing process I was experimenting with as I wrote it.

Second, I must acknowledge the intelligent, hilarious, and lovely ladies of the Between the Covers Book Club of Eastside King County, Washington. These ladies were the first in my physical reality to read *The Burial*. Their praise-laden critiques gave me the confidence and support to even try publishing this book. Whether or not my work is truly worthy of such praise is up to you to decide.

Speaking of confidence, critiques, and support, I was in a writer's group with the following people back in the day: Katie Cord, Tom Wright, Rebecca Birch, and Stephanie Weippert. The sense they gave of being part of a larger writing community has been of immense value to me over the years. They also introduced me to, or helped me get in position to meet, many other people that have been helpful sources of knowledge to me in the writing field, like Michelle Kilmer, Timothy W. Long, Jennifer Brozek, Raven Oak, Odessa Black, and others. Thanks to all of y'all!

Thanks to Cameron Smock and Dean Smith, who let me take the back cover photo and film the trailer at Washington Memorial Park in Seatac, Washington. Bonney-Watson is an excellent funeral home chain, by the way.

Thanks to all my remaining friends, specifically: Paul Tusler for pushing me to go to my father's funeral, Tommy Aiello for the fantastic back cover blurb, Amanda Matthews for hanging out on my last visit to Arkadelphia (yes, it is a real place), Helen Johnson for her help filming the trailer, and Rae Lyn Barton for listening to me whine. I had to leave out a lot of people; if this offends you, I apologize. It's late and I'm tired.

Special shouts to Gabriel Hagmann, Tanya Tuor, and my daughter Catherine for their unwavering, (mostly) unquestioning support of my insane quest to become a published, successful author.

Sierra is based on a real woman I know. I have to thank her for her friendship, support, encouragement, and being my muse for many years.

As for family, thanks to my brothers Cedric and Mark, my sister Lisa, my mother Verdina, all my scattered siblings, all my uncles alive or dead who got rolled into the character of Werner, all my aunts who might get rolled into their own character in the next book, all my cousins but especially my cousin Carolyn (RIP) who encouraged my writing from the start. Thanks and love to all of you.

Many, many thanks are due to *The Burial*'s editor, Cortney Marabetta. She kicked both this book and myself into better shape, so if you liked or hated it, it's her fault.

More thanks than words can express to my grandmother, Geneva. She was the rock of my young life; before she died, she taught me how to fight my own fears. Nothing would have been possible without that lesson. I still miss her every day, and I hope she is still watching over me.

Last but certainly not least, thanks to my father, John. I never once called him "Dad" or "Daddy" that I can remember, only John. I didn't even know his birthday until I read it on his funeral program. This book was my way of dealing with all the damage he left behind, with all the shit he put his children through. I can't say I succeeded completely in that, but I definitely made progress. Wherever you are, John, I hope you see this book. I hope you know how well I came out, and that it's as much because of you as it is in spite of you. I hope, wherever you are, that you are proud of the men and women you created, because we deserve that. This novel was the goodbye that I never got to say. Goodbye, John, rest well. For all you were and all you weren't, I love you.

Most of all, thank you for buying and reading this book. I really hope you liked it.

Pandem Buckner
June 30, 2015

The Burial

Pandem Buckner

ABOUT THE AUTHOR

Pandem grew up in the primieval woods of northern Mississippi and is just now getting around to becoming civilized. He lives somewhere around Seattle with his daughter Catherine, and spends his time doing whatever strikes his fancy at any given moment. He is also a writer, voracious reader, video game fan, comic book geek, and all-around creative machine. If you ever see him around Seattle, you probably didn't. It was just somebody that looked like him, of which there are more than you might think.

Find me!
Facebook: www.facebook.com/pandemauthor
Twitter: @PandemBuckner
YouTube: Pandem Buckner
Email: PandemBuckner@gmail.com

Pandem Buckner

Recquiescat in Pace.

Pandem Buckner

Made in the USA
San Bernardino, CA
06 July 2015